THE SECOND WAVE

Paras Over The Barras - Part 2

By James Barclay

LANG SYNE PUBLISHERS LTD.
GLASGOW

Parras over the Barras: Second Wave
was published in 1996 by Lang Syne Publishers Ltd,
Clydeway Centre, 45 Finnieston Street, Glasgow G3 8JU
and printed by Dave Barr Print, Glasgow.

I.S.B.N. 185 217 028X

*Dedicated to the Calton where I spent
my happy boyhood in it's dusty tenements...*

CHAPTER ONE

Wullie McSorley leaned out of the second-storey window and craned his neck as far as he could. The day was bright and the sun shimmered on the grey slates of the Well Street rooftops. Wullie watched a blue pigeon circle the smoking chimney pot across the street before it settled on the supporting stonework, cooing loudly his territorial rights.

To Wullie's right the trams trundled to and fro in busy London Road. Glasgow's Calton was a buzz of activity with rushing folk and tooting motors and bawling children playing in the streets.

There were sounds of leather hitting metal as they played 'Kick-the-Can'. Of victory yells of 'A-Leevo' as someone was freed from playful captivity.

Little girls had chalked 'Beds' on the pavement and sang as they skipped. Others hit ragged tennis balls off walls, raising one leg to the side and singing. 'Ladies In Tight Skirts Can't Do This!'

Wullie smiled! The children were thumbing fingers at the war! Soon enough the darkness would come down and the blackout blinds would go up. The Luftwaffe would drone overhead and the folk in the air-raid shelters would sit, tight-eyed, as a death bomb screamed down to blow to smithereens...wherever!

Daylight life went on as usual. Wullie's eyes narrowed as he saw the red bike of the post office telegram boy turn into the street from Stevenston Street. He watched as the boy scrutinized the buff envelope in his hand and scanned the closemouth numbers. Wullie wished that he would stop and felt his heart beat faster as the boy on the bike came closer.

The telegram boy braked directly under Wullie's window, glanced quickly at the envelope in his hand and then at the close...and alighted....propping his bike against the baffle wall at the edge of the pavement.

Wullie saw the boy disappear into the close and quickly came in from the window. He knew instinctively that this was a communication from the War Office...and that it concerned Big Sammy, his brother-in-law, now languishing in a German prisoner of war camp, somewhere in France.

He could hear Annie, his sister, humming quietly to herself as she tidied up the adjoining bedroom. Annie was glad that her husband was a prisoner. 'Sammy is oot o' the war..and the bullets'!

Wullie was already at the outside door before the telegram boy had a chance to knock.

The freckled-face, carrot-haired boy looked away as he handed Wullie the buff envelope. Too often had he seen tears flood as he handed over his grim communication. For grim it always was!

Wullie thanked the boy and, digging into his pocket, produced a silver threepenny-bit which he handed over to the grateful lad, who tipped the skip of his hat and muttered a 'Thanks, Mister' before hurrying down the stairs.

"Is that somebody at the door?" Annie's voice called from the bedroom.

Wullie didn't answer. He walked into the kitchen, sat at the table, sighed and tore open the envelope.

Annie, duster in hand, entered and immediately took in the scene. Her hand went to her mouth and she stifled a cry.

Wullie perused the message, looked up and held up the paper.

"It..it's aboot Sammy, int it?" Annie stammered.

Wullie nodded.

"Bad news..and good news, Annie," Wullie said to his trembling sister.

"Te..tell me the good news, Wullie," Annie said quietly..

"Big Sammy is no longer a prisoner o' the Jerries, "Wullie said. "He's escaped."

Annie let out a whoop of delight.

"Ah always knew they couldnae keep ma Sammy incar..er..incer..er.. loacked up," she cried, adding, "whit's the bad news?"

"He's noo a prisoner o' the Japs," Wullie said.

"How's that possible?" Annie said, her brows furrowing.

"Well," Wullie said, "He escaped frae the POW Camp, in France and made his wey tae Calais where he tried tae steal a boat. The Big Eejit should never have tried. He must've known he couldnae get away wi' it."

Annie shook her head.

"Naw, naw, Wullie," she said, "Any sojer who escaped and got as faur as Calais would've tried tae steal a boat."

"No' the Bismark, Annie!" Wullie said with a raised eyebrow.

"So, WHIT happened?" Annie cried.

"Well," Wullie went on, "It seems he managed tae get away again and stole a rowin' boat. But, instead o' rowin' straight across the Channel, he turned left...and was picked up."

Annie shook her head.

"He never DID have any sense o' direction," she said. "Wance, when we were in the Arcadia watchin' 'I was a Zombie's Auntie' he got up tae go for

2

ice cream and when he didnae come back Ah went tae look for him...and found him in the Olympia watching Dagwood Bumstead'.

"Aye, well he'll no' be gettin' ice-cream noo, that's for sure," Wullie said.

"Where was he picked up?" Annie said, puzzled.

"In the China Sea," Wullie said, his brows knitting, "and he was still rowin' as they were interrogatin' him in the commandant's oaffice."

"Oh, Ah hope he escapes again!" Annie said, worriedly.

"It's no' possible, Annie," Wullie said authoritatively. "He'd need tae find his wey through the jungle...he'd have nae chance!"

"Oh aye, he would!" Annie blurted, "He saw every Tarzan film that was ever made. He was obsessed wi' Tarzan, so he wis."

"Big Sammy couldnae get obsessed wi' anythin'?" Wullie sniped, "Except maybe drink."

"Is that so?" Annie retorted, "He wanted tae call oor Rita, Cheetah."

Wullie laughed. "It's no' any worse than Rasputin," he said, referring to his niece's intended.

Annie's daughter, Rita, had finally become engaged to Rasputin Plunkett, now serving with the Pioneer Corps somewhere in England.

There was still no sign of the war ending and the Luftwaffe continued to make sporadic nightly visits over Glasgow. The tenants of Well Street, in the Calton, near the 'barras', the city's famous street market, cursed the German pilots for depriving 'the weans' of their sleep....and of their education. For, after a raid, the 'weans' would be kept from school.

"Och, where is it a' gonny end?" Annie sighed. She looked over at Wullie, who was now sitting at the table reading his Bulletin.

Annie was sad that Wullie hadn't married. There had been hope when she thought that their next door neighbour Ina McLatchie had 'hooked' him. Wullie had seemed to capitulate to Ina's charms that night in the air-raid shelter when Rasputin and Rita got engaged. The same night that Big Mario Valente stormed into the shelter with a basketful of fish suppers ..thus saving the catering problem and Annie's blushes.

"Ye know, Wullie," she said at last, "Ah was very disappointed that you an' Ina didnae get engaged that night in the shelter."

"Aye, it was a near thing," Wullie said, "Ah think she must've drugged they soday scones she was feeding me wi' in the shelter. Ah lose two gallons o' sweat every time Ah think o' it!"

"Aye, well ye could dae a lot worse than Ina," Annie said, "Her poor faither noo gone an' her left all alone wi' naebody tae talk tae...whit a waste!"

Wullie slammed down his paper on top of the table.

"Noo, don't you start that matchmakin' stuff again, Annie," he cried. "And she spends hauf the night talkin' tae that windae boax."

"It's because her faither's ashes were scattered in that boax that she talks tae it." Annie said in way of mitigation.

"It's no' natural," Wullie said, "Ah've heard o' folk sittin' talkin' tae their plants. But tae sit talkin tae a boax full o' yer deid faither....!"

He was interrupted by a loud rapping at the door. Ina McLatchie hurried in.

"Ah didnae know there was an air-raid oan?" Wullie cried, jumping up.

"There's no' an air-raid on," Ina said.

"Oh, Ah just surmised there was," Wullie said "wi' you wearin' yer gas mask."

"Ah'm no' wearin ma gas mask," Ina said indignantly.

Annie scowled and Wullie, with a wry smile, turned away.

"Naw, Ah saw the telegram boy comin' up the close and Ah immediately thought the worse," Ina said, sympathy in her voice.

"It's aboot Big Sammy, intit?" she added.

Annie nodded.

"Aye, he's noo a prisoner o' the Japs." Annie said, dabbing her eyes. "Ma poor Sammy..it'll kill him. He hates rice. He'll die o' mal...mal...malpractice, so he will."

"That's the wrang word, Annie," Wullie corrected. "It's Malmunition."

"Aye, well he'll no' eat, that's for sure," Annie said.

"How did he get caught?" Ina asked, knitting her brows.

"He escaped and got caught rowin' in the China Sea," Annie replied worriedly.

"Geez, that must've been painful!" Ina cried, bringing her hand to her mouth.

Wullie shook his head and raised his eyebrows.

"C'mon, Ina, let's have a wee cuppa tea," Annie said, indicating a chair.

Annie poured out three cups of tea. Ina sipped and, looking over the lip of her cup, said:

"Imagine Sammy a prisoner of the Japs...away oot there in the tropics. You'll no' recognise him when he gets hame, Annie."

Annie shuddered.

"Ah know," she said, " he'll be that thin, ye mean?"

Ina shook her head. "Naw, he'll have a rerr tan," she said innocently, then added, "Dae ye think he'll try tae escape?"

"He might," Annie said. "the jungle's got nae fear for him. He's seen every Tarzan picture ever made."

"Imagine Big Sammy stealin' a boat and gettin' as faur as the China Sea!"Ina sighed, "it's that darin', so it is...like an Errol Flynn film."

Annie agreed. "Aye," she drooled, "only ma Sammy could've stole a boat at Calais and made it tae the China Sea."

"Ye're dead right!" Wullie exclaimed, "How the hell did he get as faur as that? That's whit Ah want tae know. He must've cerried the bloody boat right across Poland."

"Naw, naw," Annie said, jumping to her spouse's defence. "Ma Sammy was a great paddler. Every Sunday before the war we used tae go alang tae Hogganfield Loch and Sammy would paddle in it."

Wullie's eyebrows went up.

"Aye, he had nae shame," he said.

"Whit's shame got tae dae wi' it?" Annie snapped, "A' Ah said was that we used tae go tae Hogganfield Loch and Sammy liked nothing better than tae paddle in it. Whit's wrang wi' that?"

"Ah thought ye said 'piddle'," Wullie replied with a wry smile.

"He liked rowin', then?" Ina piped up.

Annie nodded. "Oh, aye! He would row up an' doon that loch for 'oors. That's probably why he ended up paddlin' in the China Sea. He didnae know when tae stop."

Annie topped Ina and Wullie's cups up and sat down, resting her hands on her lap. "It would've been lovely tae have Big Sammy hame for Hogmanay," she said dreamily. "Just tae see him walkin' in that door. He looked that handsome in his uniform!"

"Aye, an' wi' his bronzed face," Ina sighed. Then, turning to Wullie, she twittered. "Ah think you'd look wonderful in uniform, Wullie!"

Wullie's chest puffed out.

"Aye, well ye should've seen me in the last war...in ma H.L.I. kilt..the Mackenzie tartan, it was..Aye, The Lady from Hell, they called me!" Wullie said proudly.

"Was that when ye were chargin' towards the enemy ower the battle-field?" Ina asked, her jaw dropping.

"Naw, that was when he was doorman at the Calton Social Club and was chargin' too much at the door for the Setterday night dances," Annie chirped.

Wullie scowled.

"As a matter of fact," he said, "Ah see that Anthony Eden is lookin' for men up tae the age of sixty-five for to join the Local Defence Volunteers. It's in case the Jerries send ower their parachutists...like they did in Holland an' Belgium. It's tae guard the likes o' factories and power stations and railways an' that. An' we don't want Paras ower the barras either."

Ina clapped her hands together.

"Oh, are ye gonny join, then, Wullie?" she cooed.

Wullie shook his head.

"No' bloody likely!" he snapped, "They've nae guns, so they've no'. They're paradin' with brooms for rifles and wee brushes for hand guns. Some good that!"

"It be awkward right enough if you were staunin' there at Templeton's and suddenly a squad o' paratroopers landed oan the grun in front o' ye!" Ina agreed.

"Ye're no' kiddin'," Wullie grunted, "Whit are ye supposed tae dae then, eh? Step forward and brush them doon? "Welcome tae Glesca, Fritz, Here staun' still , ye're a' stoor, haud still an' Ah'll brush ye doon. An' ,if ye've got time, Ah'll poalish yer boots.Naw, ye'll no' get me joinin' 'til they get proper guns," Wullie was adamant.

"But ye'd still look nice in yer uniform," Ina said.

"Naw, Ah couldnae wear that uniform," Wullie said puckering his lips, "that khaki is faur too rough for ma skin, so it is. Ah'd come oot in a rash."

"Ho...listen tae him," Annie cried. "Wullie, the only thing that makes you come oot in a rash is when ye're asked tae put yer haun' in yer poacket and get a round up...He's the only customer in the Come Inn pub wi' three zips in his troosers...wan in the front and wan at each side."

"Aw, that's no' fair," Wullie wailed. "Ah'm mair liberal wi' ma money than Big Sammy anyway. His haun's are never in his poacket. HE gets frost-bite in his fingers."

Annie ignored him. "Here," she said,"it gets dark early these nights...better pull the blackout blinds." She rose and pulled the large black drapes together.

"Don't want tae get Erchie McPherson's hunkers up," she giggled.

Special Constable Erchie McPherson had been noticeable by his absence recently...ever since his dressing down by a superior for his Gestapo-like attitude.But his whistle was still well-tuned and any sign of a chink of light coming from a careless window during the blackout, got its full blast.

Wullie was fed up with the Luftwaffe's raids. They were disturbing his sleep and he didn't like that.

Wullie mentioned that he was considering purchasing the super Hudson Shelter. It was selling at thirty-pounds and was made in Coatbridge from "Dazlo rust-resisting plates", weighing about thirteen hundredweight. He had seen the cylindrical shelter, on show at St Enoch's Square for the public's approval. It had been given a blessing by the Home Office as suitable for four persons and would give protection against "blast and splinter." Wullie had been impressed. "It would save havin' tae jump up an dress quickly," he said.

But Annie pooh-poohed the idea. Besides she could do a lot more with thirty pounds, she reckoned.

"Auld Mrs Flemin' up the next close has wan," Wullie groaned.

"Aye, and whit good is it tae her?" Annie said, "She steys three up and she's got it in her room. Whit's the point..gettin' up oot yer bed when the sirens go, croassin' the flair intae yer shelter...it's daft!"

"We could keep it roon' the back," Wullie argued. "then, when the sirens go, it would just be a matter o' nippin' doon the stairs and no' havin' tae croass tae the pen'."

The 'Pend' was halfway down Well Street, between London Road and Stevenston Street. It was a large, cobbled expanse which housed a stable where a carter kept his horse. There was a stairway running up the outside of one of the buildings dubbed 'The Jew's Stairs' by the Well Street community because of the race of the gentleman who occupied the small factory at the top where a door led to a small upholstery repair shop.

At night the large Clydesdale horse could be heard stamping and neighing inside his stable, obviously agitated for some reason. And, in the morning, the reason for his nocturnal dance was evident when the carter arrived to open the large, green doors. Dozens of dead mice littered the ground inside...flattened by Dobbin's powerful hooves . They had paid the price of annoying the gentle giant.

Adjacent to the stable was a storeroom where a coal merchant kept bags of coal stacked up. Many a housewife going into her coal bunker, to top up the fire in her range — or, alternatively, if she was right up to date - her tiled 'interior' was in for a shock as she shovelled up the coal...and half-a-dozen dead mice mixed in with it. For the prankish children had the habit of collecting the dead rodents from the stable and packing them into the coal bags...still to be delivered to unsuspecting customers.

In the middle of this was the communal air-raid shelter, a flat topped brick building that could only serve to muffle blast and divert shrapnel. Any bomb landing near it would have flattened it and everybody inside. But it was a deluding sanctuary for the tenement residents, who hurried to its ever-open doors at the first wail of the dreaded warning that the Luftwaffe, the German Air Force, had arrived with their deadly cargo.

"It only hauds FOUR, Wullie," Annie complained,referring to the Hudson Shelter.

"You, me, Rita and Ina, here."

Wullie nodded. "Right enough, Even wi' just Ina in it by hersel' it would be overcrowded." he said sarcastically.

"Ur you suggestin' that Ah'm fat?" Ina snapped.

"Naw, naw," Annie said quickly, "Wullie didnae mean that, Ina, didn't ye no', Wullie?" she scowled.

"Let's put it this wey," Wullie said, "If she stood at the fit o' the close, we widnae need a baffle wa.'"

"Never mind him, Ina," Annie comforted, "he's an ignorant get!"

Ina smiled a weak smile. She knew Wullie and his tactics. When her father, Old Jake McLatchie died and she was suddenly free, after years of looking after him, she turned her sights to confirmed bachelor, Wullie.

For a while she thought she had trapped Wullie after he had agreed to collect her father's ashes from the undertaker and had given a homily as she scattered her old man in her window box, as was his wish.

On the night of Rita's engagement to Rasputin Plunkett, as they sat in the shelter during a raid, Wullie had actually squeezed her hand after devouring some soda scones she had baked...knowing it was his favourite delicacy.

But Wullie had gone back to his old ways and never missed a turn to throw facetious remarks at her. But Ina was determined and Wullie was not going to get off that easily.

Ina thanked Annie for the tea.

"Ah must get in and watter the windae boax," she said, turning at the door.

"It'll no' bring yer faither back," Wullie sniped.

Ina ignored him and closed the door quietly behind her.

Annie switched on the wireless and sighed as Bing Crosby's voice flooded the room with 'Don't Fence Me In'.

Outside, a happy pigeon cooed and the rumble of the 'caurs' clanged along busy London Road. Wullie wondered if Jerry would be over this night? If he would be dashing across the street and up the 'pen'?

Rita had checked in her cash at the Ruby Street tram depot. She had just finished work on the Number Nine tram — Scotstoun to Auchenshuggle, and had managed to get a meal of pie and chips at the National Restaurant, in Gallowgate where she had made her way down to make sure that the Barrowland Dance Hall would be opened that weekend. For there was a rumour that it had been ordered to close its doors until further notice. Satisfied that the scare was untrue and things would be going on as normal she took advantage of the National Restaurant and so saved Annie from preparing a meal.

She crossed the road and walked up Kent Street before turning into London Road, on past St Alphonsus' Chapel and on towards Well Street. She stopped at Margaret Forrester's shop at the corner of London Road and Bain Street and sighed as her eyes caught the white satin wedding dress in the dimmed window.

"If only Rasputin could get some leave!" she thought. The picture of the wedding dress stayed in her mind as she dreamily walked on.

"Ah, ye're hame!" Annie exclaimed as Rita walked in and slumped on to a chair.

"Had a busy day, hen?" Annie went on as she fussed over a basin of hot water to which she had added a liberal amount of dried, English mustard.

She placed the basin at Rita's feet...now bare after she had kicked off her shoes and peeled off her stockings.

"Oh, that's Heaven, mammy!" she said wearily, slipping her feet into the comforting warmth.

"You just let them soak, hen," Annie said, patting her shoulder. "Whit would ye like tae eat?"

"Nothin', Mammy," Rita said, "Ah managed tae get somethin' in the National, in the Gallygate."

"Nae Mario's fish suppers the night then?" Wullie said, looking up from his paper.

"Naw, no' the night...and nae Barraland the night either," she sighed. "It's no'the same with Raspy away fightin' for his country. Ah just wanted tae know if it would be open at the weekend."

"He'll no' be daein' much fightin' in Aldershot," Wullie said sarcastically.

Rita ignored her uncle's sarcasm.

"Oh mammy," she cried, "ye should see the weddin' dress they've got in Margaret Forrester's windae...oh, it's just lovely!"

"Nae doot ye'd need a lot o' clothin' coupons hen," Annie said.

"Probably....but it would be worth it," Rita sighed.

"Never you mind, hen," Annie said, putting an arm around her daughter's shoulder and giving an affectionate squeeze, "this war canny last forever."

"Ah widnae say that," Wullie piped up, "Noo that Rasputin's in the army it might just last twice as long."

"Don't you dare say anythin' aboot ma fiance," Rita snapped. "He's tryin' his best. Already he's asked for a meetin' wi General Montgomery tae put his plans tae him for endin' the war. It's just that he hasn't heard back frae him."

"He's got a better chance gettin' a reply frae Hitler," Wullie sniped.

"Ah just wish he'd get a leave," Rita said, "Ah'm dyin tae see him in uniform. He could wear it at the weddin'. Ah can just see us noo...walkin' doon the aisle ..me takin' his airm."

"You'll just need tae take his haun' or he'll have tae wear a pair o' stilts."

"He's no' that tall," Rita cried.

"He's a' legs and nae brains," Wullie said. "He's somewhere in between a genius and an idiot and leaning towards the latter. No' that tall? He's the only man that can clean Granny Black's windaes withoot usin' a ladder."

"Och, you've always got somethin' tae say, Wullie," Annie said reprovingly. "Whit's Granny Black's windae got tae dae wi' anythin'?"

"She steys three up," Wullie said smugly.

"Never you mind him, hen," Annie said, pecking Rita's cheek. "Rasputin's daein' his bit...mair than Ah can say for some folk!" Wullie didn't miss the dagger thrown.

"An' we received news aboot yer faither the day," Annie went on. Rita sat bolt upright.

"He..He..He's no' deid, is he?" she stammered.

"Naw, he's a prisoner o' the Japs," Annie said, dabbing her eye.

Rita's jaw dropped open.

"Have the Japs occupied France?" she asked in disbelief.

"Naw, he escaped frae the French camp an' stole a boat at Calais and, instead o' rowin' straight across the Channel, he decided tae turn left and God only knows whit other diversions he found but, anywey, he ended up paddlin' in the China Sea and was picked up," Wullie said, glorying in his narrative.

"Bu..But that's terrible!" Rita cried."He hates rice. It turns him a funny colour. Aw, whit a shame!"

Wullie laid his paper down on the table. "Personally," he began, "Ah think he escaped and made his wey tae Calais and he deliberately turned right and headed for the China Sea. Somebody in the camp probably telt him how tae get there."

"Who would tell him that?" Annie asked, knitting her brows.

"Probably a German guard," Wullie said.. "probably gled tae get rid o' him."

"But whit would he tell him that would make him want tae go a' that distance?" Annie wailed.

"Probably telt him he'd be in amongst a lot o' nips," Wullie replied with a wry grin."An' Sammy loves his nips."

"Och away ye go," Annie said, giving him a playful clout.

"Ah was hopin' he'd escape an' gie me away at ma weddin'?" Rita said ruefully.

"Ye never know yer luck," Wullie said, "The Japs might just throw him oot and, ye never know, he might just turn up wan o' these days at the close, ridin' an elephant."

"Just like Sabu!" Rita exclaimed.

"Aye, only a different colour," Wullie grinned.

"Depends how much rice he's ate," Rita said

They had a good laugh and Rita decided finally to go to bed. She had an early rise and was on the number eighteen run. Green cars go east and the run, between Burnside and Springburn, was always a busy one...especially if the greyhounds were running at Shawfield where the tram passed.

She wondered what Rasputin was doing at that particular moment and hoped he would get a leave soon.Rasputin had said that he was trying to get a meeting with Mister Churchill, the Prime Minister, to give him some ideas on how to end the war. But not only was he finding it difficult to get near him, he was finding it difficult to get past the corporal who would not even allow him to see his commanding officer. Rita lay down, hoping the Luftwaffe would allow her a full night's rest. She thought of her father and hoped he was not suffering too much. Rita closed her eyes and smiled to herself. She was thinking of Margaret Forrester's...and the beautiful wedding dress in the window.

Rita could hear loud snoring coming from Wullie's bedroom when she rose in the morning. It was a dull day and light rain tapped on the window. She jumped up from bed, stretched and, slipping on an old house coat, ambled into the kitchen.

As usual, Annie was already up and dressed. The kettle on, the gas ring was boiling.

"Oh, ye're up, hen!" Annie exclaimed. "Hang on, Ah'll just pour this intae the basin."

Annie placed the enamelled basin in the sink and filled it up with water from the kettle. "There ye are, hen," she said.

Rita thanked her mother and washed herself in the warm water. The carbolic soap stung her eyes and she let out a yelp.Annie immediately handed her a clean towel saying, "Noo you go an' get ready and Ah'll have yer porrage ready an' a wee bit toast, eh?"

Rita smiled and vanished into the bedroom. She was out again within minutes, dressed in the smart, green uniform of the Glasgow Corporation tram car conductress.

"My, ye don't half look lovely in yer uniform," Annie said proudly.

"Och, mammy, ye say that EVERY mornin', so ye dae," Rita said, a little embarrassed.

"An' why not?" Annie replied.

Rita shook her head and sat down at the table. Annie switched on the wireless and began to hum in unison with Carrol Gibbons and his Orchestra playing 'Smoke Gets in Your Eyes'.

A quick peck on her mum's cheek and Rita was hurrying down the stairs and into the street.

She hurried up towards London Road and, for a brief moment, was tempted to turn right towards Bain Street and have another look at the dress in Margaret Forrester's window. But there was no time. She turned left and went into Mr Adams' newsagent shop and purchased her Daily Record and five cigarettes...three Woodbine and the obligatory two Pasha. She would give the Turkish cigarettes away to one of the drivers. She wondered why it was that she could not get FIVE Woodbine in the packet and what it was that the Turkish government had on the British government that demanded they put two of their smelly, obnoxious cigarettes in with the sweet smelling Virginia tobacco? Nobody could answer that and smokers were now glad to get what they could. But Rita demanded that none of her passengers light up the stinking weed on any of HER 'caurs'.

She hurried on to the tram stop in London Road, at Claythorn Street and jumped on to a number twenty-six, which would take her up Dalmarnock Road and drop her at the Ruby Street tram depot.

Forty minutes later her 'caur' swung into Elmbank Street, on its way to Springburn. At the top of the street loomed the impressive Beresford Hotel building, standing tall and majestic in Sauchiehall Street. The Stars and Stripes fluttered in the morning breeze from the flagpole and already a dozen or so G.I.'s were milling around the doors.

American soldiers were billeted in the Beresford Hotel...and happy to be so. A hundred yards down the road was The Locarno Ballroom. Nice and easy staggering distance. And while many of the G.I.'s enjoyed the luxury of that dancehall, many still preferred to head east to Barrowland where they could let their hair down in the 'Jitterbugging' corner.

Some of the Yanks gave Rita a wave as her car turned left towards Charing Cross and, smiling broadly, she waved back, her driver, Big Tam, giving a few loud clangs on his foot bell.

Rita smiled to herself. "These lads have still to experience a Glasgow Hogmanay," she thought. "Only one week to go!" She wondered if Rasputin would get home for the celebrations? She hoped so.

Rita checked in her bag and cash that night. The day had been uneventful and she was glad to get finished. She jumped on to a number nine car, going to Scotstoun, at Bridgeton Cross and stayed on until one stop past her stop. Yes, the dress was still in the shop window. Rita sighed and turned for home.

Annie had the basin of warm water and mustard all ready for her daughter when she arrived.

Rita flopped on to the chair by the roaring fire, kicked her shoes off and rolled down her heavy stockings. She sighed as she allowed her aching feet to slide slowly into the comforting warm water.

"Aw, you're a gem, Mammy!" she sighed.

"A busy day, hen?" Annie asked.

"Naw, no' really," Rita said, "But the toon's teemin' wi' Yanks."

"Ach, they're jist boys, maist o' them," Annie said, her maternal instinct swelling up.

"Where's Uncle Wullie?" Rita asked, noting that Wullie was not in his usual seat reading his Evening Times.

"Oh, he's away arranging for his cairry-oot for Hogmanay tae be uplifted," Annie laughed.

"Already?" Rita said, raising her eybrows. "Away doon tae the Come Inn pub?" she queried.

"Naw, Pickfords," Annie said.

The two women laughed. In pre-war days it might have just taken Pickfords, the furniture removers, to collect Wullie and Big Sammy's 'Cairry-oot' for Hogmanay. But not now.

The outside door slamming shut made them turn round. Wullie charged in, flopped on to a chair and sat, his fingers drumming on the table top. Wullie was obviously angry.

"Whit's up wi' you, then?" Annie said.

"Wan hauf boattle, that's a' they're gonny gie me," Wullie cried, "Efter a' the business Ah've gied them ower the years. WAN hauf boattle o' Johnny Walker and that's ma lot. Whoever heard o' anybody bringin' in the New year wi' wan lousy hauf boattle, eh?"

He buried his head in his hands. Annie put an understanding arm around his shoulders.

"Never mind, Wullie," she commiserated, " "Jist think o' the good ye're daein' yer liver."

"Ma liver," Wullie said, almost weeping, "was brought up on whisky. It demands it...jist like a baby demands milk. Ah blame ma maw, so Ah dae. When Ah used tae wake up durin' the night, greetin' and screamin', she used tae dip ma tit intae a boattle o' whisky tae send me tae sleep again. Then as time went oan, Ah insisted wearin' a tile hat tae school...and no' only that, Ah was expelled for bein' drunk a' the time. Ma maw was ashamed o' me."

"Nae wonder," Annie said, "Ye were only five at the time."

"Aye, well Ah'm no' takin' this lyin' doon," Wullie said, "Ah doot this is another joab that only wan man in the whole o' Calton can sort oot....Fingers McGeachie."

Wullie put his hand to his heart and spoke Fingers McGeachie's name with a true reverence. If anybody could help stock up Wullie's cairry-oot it would be Fingers.

"Dae ye think Fingers could get his haun' on some claethes coupons Uncle Wullie?" Rita said, drying off her feet.

"Ye don't need claeths coupons for bevvy,"Wullie said.

"No' for bevvy," Rita cried, "For a weddin' dress."

Wullie turned.

"Are ye really gonny mairry that idiot?" he snapped.

"Rasputin is not an idiot, Uncle Wullie," Rita retorted, "Right noo Ah can see him sittin' talkin' wi' General Montgomery discussin' tactics."

"Ah didnae know that Monty played Ludo," Wullie sniped.

"Oh mammy, listen tae him," Rita wailed, "Callin' ma Raspy an idiot."

"Never mind him, hen," Annie comforted, "At least he's a sober idiot. HE didnae get chucked oot o' school for being stoned."

Rita said nothing. She knew that Wullie had a sneaking admiration for her fiance and was just depressed. Annie turned and took her coat from the peg on the door.

"Ah'm just goin' doon tae the factor's", she said, "Auld Granny Black's havin terrible trouble wi' dampness and that auld midden, Campbell, the factor, has ignored her protests. But he'll no' ignore her noo. She came a' oot in warts and had tae go tae the doactor."

"Whit's that got tae dae wi' her dampness?" Rita asked, "Dampness don't gie ye warts."

"It wisnae warts," Annie said, "the auld sowel had mushrooms."

"Ach, Ah don't believe it," Wullie snapped, "Ye don't grow mushrooms oan yer boady."

"If the hoose is damp enough, ye dae," Annie retorted."Auld Granny Black is a walkin' fungus."

Annie hurried out and Rita and Wullie's eyes met...and they burst out laughing.

"Yer maw talks some rubbish at times!" Wullie said.The blast from a warden's whistle made him jump and check the blackout blind. Everything was in order. He turned the wireless on and nearly wept as The Andrews Sisters sang lustily... 'Roll Out The Barrel'.

The thought of a dry Hogmanay swept over him once again.

CHAPTER TWO

The sound of the letter box snapping made Rita jump from bed. It might be a letter from Rasputin. She threw on her housecoat and hurried through. She jumped with joy and held the letter to her heart as she recognised Rasputin's handwriting.Rita hurried through to her bedroom, threw herself on top of the bed and tore the envelope open. She wanted to be alone when she read her fiance's communication.

'My Darlin' Rita',the letter began, 'Ah have just finished negotiations wi' the general and he was very impressed wi' ma plans for ending the war.

'In fact, efter Ah had finished talking, he was so impressed that he said Ah should go on leave and get merried...and Ah could stay on leave as long as Ah like. Ah think he thought Ah was parted frae you for too long, 'cos he said he was sorry for you. Wasn't that nice?

'And so, my wee lamb, Ah'll be hame for Hogmanay. The General was so good aboot it a' that he sent the sergeant major personally doon tae the railway station tae make sure Ah got a ticket.

'No' only that', 'he has gied me a special uniform for to get married in. He said it was smarter and mair pertainin' tae whit he saw me in. Ah won't put any kisses at the end o' this letter...'cos I've got a bad cauld'. Your loving genius, Rasputin. P.S. 'Ah have just been awarded a medal.'

Rita's heart leapt.A medal! HER Rasputin, in the army just a matter of weeks and awarded a medal already. Her heart swollen with pride, Rita leapt from the bed and hurried into the room.

"Raspy's been awarded a medal," she cried. Annie was caught up in Rita's joy. "Oo, a medal!" she cried, clapping her hands.

"That's amazin'," Wullie said, "a medal and he's never been oot o' Aldershot. Whit medal did he get?"

Rita held up the letter and scrutinized it closely. "Ah can hardly make it oot," she said screwing up her eyes, "It..it's something Cross."

"It widnae be the Victoria Cross, would it?" Annie cried. Wullie shook his head. "Nae chance!" he said, "Ye only get that for valour. No' for pallor."

Ina, who had come in after picking up Wullie's morning paper from Mr Adams' shop, in London Road, clapped her hands together and jumped for joy; "Ooh, a medal," she cooed.

"D'ye think it could really be the Victoria Cross?" Annie asked with pride.

"Annie, ye don't get the Victoria Cross squarebashin' in Aldershot," Wullie sneered.

"Aw, Ah see it noo!" Rita yelled, "It...it's The IRON CROSS, First Class!"

Wullie threw up his arms. "WHIT?" he yelled, "THAT is a bloody German decoration. Whit general has he been negotiatin' wi'...bloody ROMMEL?"

Annie immediately jumped to her future son-in-law's defence.

"The boy means well," she said softly.

"Jist think," Ina said, "he'll be able tae wear his medal at the weddin'!"

"Ah am definitely no' walkin' doon the aisle tae hand her ower tae a bloke wearing the Iron Cross," Wullie snapped.

"It's aboot time you were walkin' doon the aisle yersel'," Annie said, "When are ye gonny tie the knot, anywey?"

"As faur as SHE'S concerned," Wullie said, nodding towards Ina, "wance Ah get a suitable rope."

Ina gave him a playful nudge.

""Ah'll string along with you, Wullie," she smiled.

"An' Ah'll string you up," Wullie said.

Annie felt sorry for Ina. Her life was lonely since she lost her father and Wullie's continual spurning of her made Annie mad.

"Ye must miss yer faither oot the hoose, Ina," Annie said, giving Ina McLatchie's arm a squeeze.

Ina sighed. "Oh, aye," she said quietly, "Ah sat doon the other night and flicked through his Hollywood scrapbook...when he was ower there making that picture wi' Rin-Tin- Tin, the wonder dug. He had on a lovely pair of yella and purple troosers an' a green, silk shirt an' a big, blue cowboy hat that Gene Autry gave him. An' he was jist sittin' there in the sunshine smokin' his pipe."

Annie shook her head. "That's terrible," she said, "dressin' a dug up like that."

Ina laughed. "Naw, naw, it was ma DA' dressed up."

Annie blushed. "Daft me!" she said.

"Youse will be getting geared up for Hogmanay?" Ina said, pushing her father out of her thoughts.

Annie nodded.

"Aye, but Ah'm gonny be busy. The hoose has got tae be tidied up and Ah was gonny go tae the steamie an' Ah've a dumplin' tae make....Wullie loves dumplin".

"A dumplin' for a dumplin'," Ina grinned. Wullie drew her a contemptuous look but said nothing.

"And it's ma turn o' the stairs," Annie went on, "and Ah was just wonderin' if that auld wash hoose roon' the back court was still workin'. It's been years since Ah tried it. It would be rerr and handy just tae nip doon there and bung the claeths in the auld boiler. Ah used tae use it a lot when Sammy was here, before the war," Annie said, her mind going back, "It was great! Intae the biler wi' them and an auld wumman used tae come roon' the back and sing 'Nellie Dean'. Ye were serenaded while ye worked. Ah must find oot if the biler's still workin'. It would save me a lot of time!"

"No' only that,"Ina said, "Ye could stick yer dumplin' in the biler as well."

"That's right," Annie cried.

"Och, well. Ah'll leave ye to it, mammy," Rita said, "Ah was gonny go tae Barraland the night but, noo that Ah know that Raspy could walk in any minute, Ah'd better no'. Ah'll away in and lie doon an' read ma letter again."

"Aye, you dae that, hen," Annie said, "Dream aboot yer love. Ah can only dream aboot mine. Ah can see yer faither noo...somewhere in the jungle. Lyin' doon on his straw bed and knowin' that we're a' preparin' for Hogmanay. Who'll be oor first foot an' that? Somebody tall an' dark, we hope...for luck!" Annie sighed.

"True enough!" Ina said, "Ah mean HIS First Fit could be a gorilla."

"God forbid!" Annie cried, "It would be a massacre".

"Aye, God help the bloody gorilla, "Wullie said. "Especially if Sammy's got a drink in him. He just disnae like animals, your Sammy."

"Whit makes ye say that?" Annie said with indignation.

"Well, mind the time we went tae Wilson's Zoo, in Oswald Street, and Sammy loast the heid when that poor animal, jist following its natural instincts, grabbed that banana aff him."

"Whit did he dae?" Ina asked curiously.

"He gave the poor dumb brute a hidin'. Left it flat oot and semi-conscious. We got chucked oot an' told no' tae come back."

"Whit a shame!" Ina said with concern. "Was it a wee playful monkey?"

"Naw, it was a lion," Wullie said flatly.

Ina's jaw dropped as the door was suddenly battered by an authoritative rap.

"Ah'll get it," Ina cried from the bedroom. Voices were heard coming from the lobby and Erchie McPherson entered. Removing his tin hat, he wiped his brow.

"It's gonny be wan o' these nights!" the Special Constable said, flopping on to a chair. "Jerry might just come ower to demoralise us seein' we've got the hoaliday spirit!"

"Ye'd think they'd gie us a break seein' it's nearly Hogmanay," Annie said, chewing her lip.

"Oh, aye, sure!" Wullie snapped, "Ah can just see Goering linin' up his pilots. "Noo, seein' it's nearly Hogmanay," he says, "Ah want for youse tae go ower there the night an' drap some bevvy."

Erchie threw Wullie a contemptuous look.

"It might be yersel' that'll be oor First Fit, Erchie?" Annie smiled.

Erchie shook his head.

"Nae chance, Annie," he said, "Ah wull be on duty the night. We are oot for tae protect youse in case of invasion. Also for tae keep oor trained eyes on public hooses where it has been known for certain elements of the criminal fraternity for to enter efter closing 'oors when said pubs are shut for the night. Also it is ma duty for tae warn youse that during last night's air-raid, a bomber was shot doon and the pilot seen for tae bale oot....and he still hisnae been captured. A dangerous situation!"

Annie clutched her heart and flopped on to a chair and spreadeagled her legs.

"Thank God you're oot there, Erchie, protectin' us yins..! Ah thought we'd a' be too drunk tae notice the Germans comin' doon on their parachutes for to attack us". Erchie failed to see the mischievous twinkle in Annie's eye.

"And dae other terrible things tae us while we're drunk," Ina said, knitting her eyebrows.

"It's THEM that would need tae be drunk tae dae any other things tae YOU!" Wullie sneered.

"It definitely gies us comfort for to know that you are oot there, Erchie!" Annie repeated.

"Baton at the ready!" Erchie said, with a slight puff of the chest.

Annie smiled. "We'll be safe in oor stupor," she said.

"Ah'll ALWAYS be there for to protect YOU, Annie," Erchie sighed.

Annie poured out the tea and Erchie sipped.

"Whit's the latest oan Big Sammy?" he said, smacking his lips.

"He is noo hittin' the saké," Wullie said with knowledge.

"Geez, Ah didnae know you was psychic, Wullie," Erchie said mockingly. "Ye can tell that Big Sammy, away in France in a P.O.W. Camp, is aboot tae get intae his bed?"

"Ach, Ah don't know whether he's goin' intae his bed or no'," Wullie growled, "Ah meant he wull be drinkin Saké this Hogmanay...'cos he's in the jungle wi' the Nips."

Erchie nodded knowingly.

"Aye, well, where the nips are, ye'll find Sammy."

Annie dabbed her eyes. "Ye don't understaun', Erchie," she sobbed, "Ma Sammy is noo a prisoner o' the Japanese...ma poor man!"

"Ach Ah widnae say that," Erche said, "Saké's no' that bad, Ah've tasted it."

"Ah'm no' talkin' aboot that,"Annie snapped. "It's the fact that ma Sammy is oot there somewhere in the jungle...loacked up in a bamboo hut hatin' rice."

"Bamboo hut for a bampot!" Wullie sniped. Annie scowled.

Ina saw Annie's distress and immediately changed the subject.

"Dae ye think there'll be an air-raid the night, Erchie?" she said.

Erchie shrugged.

"Ah am not cognizant wi' Hitler's plans," he said, "But, if Ah hear screamin' comin' frae your bedroom, Ina, Ah wull know that they wull have landed."

Ina sighed. "Ah wull scream as loud as Ah can, Erchie," she twittered.

"Ah meant if Ah hear wan o' THEM screamin'", Erchie said.

"They widnae invade on the night before Hogmanay surely," Annie volunteered.

"Oh aye they would!" Erchie answered. "It would be the ideal time for them tae come....knowin' what state hauf o' Glesca would be in at this time o' the year. Wan o' them could be yer First Fit...or First Jackboot!"

"Oooh!" Ina cooed. A loud knock on the door made everyone freeze.

"Ah'll get it?" Rita called. Voices could be heard coming from the lobby and Curdy McVey swept in.

"Happy New Year everybody!" he slurred, swinging a bottle of V.P. wine above his head.

"Ye're too early, Curdy," Annie said.

"Ah thought you'd be in the army by noo," Erchie said, "Are ye still working for the undertaker's?"

Curdy nodded. "Aye, Ah am still plantin' them," he said irreverently.

Turning to Ina, he muttered, "How's your faither?"

"He's still deid," Ina said and dabbed her eye.

"Aye," Curdy said, "that's the tragedy o' it. Noo, listen, Ah know Ah'm drunk but there's a good reason for it. An auld wumman in Claythorn Street wi' nae relatives died yesterday and Ah was sent alang tae the wake. Noo, Ah didnae mind that. The auld sowel was jist lyin' there when Ah went intae the hoose. Well, naebody else turned up...no' a neighbour...naebody. Ah felt sorry for her and Ah sat wi' her the whole night. It was a shame, so it was! Ah sat there by her bedside and held her haun'. Ah just felt it only right."

"Well, that was awfu' good of ye, Curdy," Annie said, "Ye are definitely in the right profession....full o' compassion!"

Curdy sadly shook his head.

"When Ah think o' it!" he said, "she was just lyin' there. Her auld cley pipe restin' on the sideboard. Ah thought she might like tae meet her maker wi' it, so Ah put it in her wee cauld hauns.

"Ah couldnae find a sheet or a towel tae cover her pale, deathly face, so Ah covered it wi' a Noon Record that was lyin' there. Then Ah stood tae attention wi' ma haun' on ma heart and sang, 'Abide wi' Me'. Sad, so it was!"

Annie felt a tear coming to her eye.

"Ah think it was awfu' good o' ye...gien' up yer time tae sit a' night wi' an auld wumman ye didnae even know."

"Ah fell asleep still haudin' her haun'," Curdy said.

"Did ye have tae cover her face because it's the reverent thing tae dae in the circumstances?" Ina innocently asked.

Curdy shook his head.

"Naw, it was because she was an ugly auld bitch," he said. "Ah woke up in the mornin' and the auld swine was sittin' up in bed, smokin' her pipe an' pickin' hoarses oot the paper."

"How was that?" Ina asked, her jaw dropping.

"Ah was in the wrang bloody hoose," Curdy wailed. "She thanked me for keepin' her company a' night and telt me Ah was a rerr singer and would Ah dae a quick chorus of 'Why Did You Make Me Care' before Ah left."

"An' did ye?" Ina asked.

"Naw, Ah didnae know that song so Ah did a quick tap dance an' whistled Roll Out The Barrel and got aff ma mark. Ah've been drinkin' a' mornin tae make me forget. Ah thought Ah'd missed the bells and came up tae wish youse a happy new year."

"Ach well, it was a nice thought anywey, Curdy", Annie said.

Rita entered looking like a million dollars. She knew Rasputin could arrive at any moment and she wanted to be prepared. She didn't have long to wait. A loud knock on the door made her jump.

"Ah'll get it!" Annie said, hurrying from the room. Seconds later she was back, smiling broadly.

"It's Rasputin!" she cried, "and he's wearing his new uniform."

Rita's heart leapt as her tall Adonis strode, smiling into the room. Wullie spluttered.

"Oh, God!" he exclaimed.

Rasputin was wearing the uniform of a corporal in the Wermacht, the German army. His Iron Cross, First Class, glinted in the electric light.

"Oh, ye look that handsome in yer uniform!" Rita cried, throwing her arms round him and kissing him passionately.

Rasputin grinned.

"It was gied to me by General Montgomery hisel'. Efter hearin' my plans tae end the war, he said Ah should really be wearin' this snazzy uniform...he's a real gentleman!"

Annie immediately put the kettle on and brewed up the tea. Rasputin leaned back and sipped slowly.

"We'll get married as soon as possible, Rita!" he said, squeezing her hand. "The general telt me that HE would never have thought o' usin' elephants in a grand assault and that only somebody wi' a brain like mine could've thought aboot it. Then he ordered the sergeant major tae arrange special leave for me."

"Ye look right handsome in yer uniform!" Rita said with pride in her voice. "Ah must show ye aff. Whit aboot goin' tae Barraland the night, eh? Billy McGregor's got a new singer."

Rasputin yawned. "Ah widnae mind lyin' doon for a wee while," he said, "Ah've been travellin' for 'oors."

"Right, then!" Rita said,"Up ye come. Ye can lie doon on tap o' ma bed and have forty winks." Rasputin stood up and stretched. He stifled a yawn. "Soon YOU'LL be able tae join me..in bed, Ah mean," he said shyly. Rita giggled. "C'Mon," she said, steering him out of the room.

"Well, that's that!" Annie said, "Rita's got HER man hame beside her."

"She'll no' have him long if he goes oot dressed like that!" Wullie sniped.

"General Montgomery knows whit he's daein'," Annie answered, switching the wireless on. The sound of the Crazy Gang singing 'We're Gonna Hang Out Our Washing on the Siegfried Line" blasted out.

Annie was happy to see the joy in her daughter's face and she thought of Big Sammy, languishing in a Japanese prison camp. Annie sighed.

"Ah know whit ye're thinkin', Annie," Ina said softly, squeezing her arm. Annie smiled and came back to earth as the title of the song hit her... "hang out the washing..."Ah'd better dae the stairs," she said, "then Ah can get on wi' the washin'."

Annie put the kettle on the gas ring and retrieved the pipe clay and Dettol from under the sink. Always meticulous, it took her a good hour to clean the stone stairs. They were spotless when she was finished and the smell of strong disinfectant swept all the way down to the close and into the street.

Erchie McPherson had volunteered to go down to the backcourt wash house and get the boiler going.

"Are ye sure ye'll be a'right in that backcourt wash hoose?"Ina said with concern in her voice.

"Och aye!" Annie said, "it'll no' take long tae get this lot done." She dragged the full basket load over to the door.

"Don't forget yer dumplin'," Ina said, handing her the heavy tea towel.

"Ah'd better no'!" Annie said, placing it on top of the clothes basket

"Just watch you don't put yer dumplin' in alang side Wullie's underwear," Ina laughed.

"Don't worry," Annie said, "Ah widnae want us a' tae get poisoned!"

Rita entered humming to herself. Her man was resting and he was HOME!

"That's Raspy sleepin'?" Rita said

"He's been sleepin' for years!" Wullie sniped. Rita ignored the jibe. "Oh, he looks lovely in his new uniform, so he does," she said dreamily.

"Rita, are you sure he joined the right bloody army?" Wullie said, pulling down his brows.

"The general picked oot that uniform for him," Rita said proudly, "Ah think he wants him tae get noticed!"

"Ah think he wants him tae get shot!" Wullie said.

"Ignore him, Rita," Annie said, scowling at Wullie, "Rasputin is a genius. He can talk to the animals and that's a rare gift.That's how he's gettin' a' they elephants tae help us win the war. He can talk elephant."

"Ma da' could talk tae the animals," Ina piped up.

"Aye, he spoke pigeon English," Wullie sneered.

"Listen," Ina said, turning on Wullie, "when ma da' was oot in Hollywood, makin' that film wi' Rin-Tin-Tin, they were THAT close that ma da' learned tae talk dug, so there!"

Ina stood up straight and defiantly folded her arms.

"Anybody can talk dug," Wullie sniped, "A's ye have tae say is 'woof-woof' an' haud oot yer haun'."

"Ah, but there's mair tae it than that," Ina retorted,"Ma faither built up a rapport wi' the animals. When he was makin' Tarzan and The Hungry Lion, he learned tae talk lion."

"That's because Tarzan couldnae understaun' a word he was sayin'", Wullie growled.

"Everybody in the studio were amazed when they saw ma da' and the lion in deep conversation. The two o' them got on that well that the lion would let ma faither stick his leg right in its mooth."

"Aye, he was always puttin' his fit in it, your faither!" Wullie sneered. Ina ignored him.

"Then, sadly, wan day he fell oot wi' the lion and they just stopped talkin' tae each other. It was the end of a beautiful friendship!" Ina said with a lump in her throat.

"Aw, whit a shame!" Annie piped in, "Whit did he stop talkin' tae it for?"

"It bit his leg aff." Ina said, stifling a sob..."but it didnae stop him frae workin'," she quickly added. "He got signed up for Long John Silver."

"Ah suppose that he then started talkin' parrot fashion?" Wullie said facetiously.

"Ach, you just staun' there an' talk rubbish," Annie sniped.

"Maybe so," Wullie retorted, "but Ah'm staunin' oan TWO legs."

Annie sighed. "Oh, well," she said, "Ah suppose Ah'd better get doon tae the backcourt and get this washin' done!"

Every tenement had its backcourt wash house...a communal flat topped little building with a built in boiler. Few women used it for their weekly washing although it was handy and had cemented clothes poles in the backcourt for drying. Most women preferred to go to the public wash house, 'The Steamie' where for a few coppers, they had plenty of hot water and well maintained boilers and driers...not forgetting the camaraderie when they could get a good 'blether'.

But the back court wash house was good in an emergency and Annie decided to make use of it this time for convenience sake.

"Erchie will be wonderin' whit's keepin' me," she said steering her basket towards the door. But she stopped in her tracks when she heard a commotion in the lobby. Erchie McPherson was protesting loudly at something or somebody. There were shouts and Erchie came bursting through the door into the room, his hands held high above his head. The tall, blond man behind him shoved him harder, sending him sprawling across the kitchen table. Ina's hand came up to her mouth when she saw the pistol the blond man was wielding.

"He..hee..he's that German pilot everybody's lookin' for," Erchie stammered. "He was hidin' in the wash hoose."

Wullie jumped to his feet and rolled up his sleeves.

"Hey, whit's the gemme?" he snapped making a move towards the German pilot. But the gun came up and Wullie stopped in his tracks.

"YOU...you shut up. All of you vill please be sitted down." It was a command and all obeyed. Ina was mesmerised by the airman's striking appearance. He was tall, blond and flashed blue eyes that sent her quivering more than the gun he held. His black leather jacket had the silver German eagle on its breast.

The man flopped down on to a chair at the table, his Luger sweeping across the room keeping them well covered.

"You wull never get away wi' this!" Erchie said weakly.Then, turning to Annie and Ina, added, "He would've jumped on you two the minute ye went in the wash hoose, y'know!"

"Ooh!" Ina quivered "Imagine that! Poor wee defenceless me would've had for tae surrender."

"You would've surrendered tae Frankenstein if he had been in there," Wullie sniped. "Noo, listen, you," he said, stabbing a finger at their captor and finding new courage, "Any messin' aboot and Ah will have tae send for the boys."

"Vot boys is zat, zen?" the German sneered.

"Ra boys...the Glesca gang boys. They make your S.S. men look like altar boys. You'd best no tangle wi' them...the San Toi, frae Calton, the Billy Boys, frae Brigton and the Baltic Fleet, frae Baltic Street...near the Ruby Street caur depot."

The German jumped to his feet.

"Mein Gott!" he said excitedly, "Ze Baltic Fleet is HERE?"

Wullie nodded. "Aye, alang wi' the Billy Boys, the San Toi an' no' forgettin' the Govan an' Possil boys...so, you be careful."

The German could not take this in. His mind was racing.

"You haff ze Baltic Fleet tied up HERE, in Glasgow?" he said with incredulity.

"Ve haff!" Wullie said.

"Ze Fuehrer must hear of zis immediatly. He vos vondering ver ze Baltic Fleet vos holed up.. I vill get ze Iron Cross for zis."

"Her boyfriend's got wan o' them," Ina said, pointing to Rita. The big German ignored her.

"I feel like a drink!" the pilot said.

"So dae Ah but it's rationed and this is nearly Hogmanay," Wullie said.

"Haff you any schnapps?" The man with the gun snapped.

"Only the wans we got took at Rothesay last year," Annie said innocently.

"Aw, gie the man some schnapps," Wullie said with a plea.

"Eh?" Annie's brows went up.

"Ye know...they schnapps we were savin' for the bells."

"Ah, you haff Bells, ja?," the German said, his eyes lighting up. "A goot Scotch whisky, zat."

"Naw, naw," Wullie said, "the bells bringin' in the new year...no' the whisky bells. We've nane o' that. Gie him some schnapps, Annie."

Annie loooked puzzled.

"Ah you do haff schnapps,eh?" the German said,

"Ve haff," Wullie said, "You must forgive Annie. We don't call it schnapps, y'see."

"Oh, and vot do you call it, mm?" the pilot said, his brows knitting.

"We call it paraffin," Wullie said.

"Ah, paraffin!" the German said, his eyes widening.

"Aye, paraffin. Gie oor guest a gless o' paraffin, Annie," Wullie ordered. "The good stuff..that stuff we got in the drysalter's."

Annie winked and turned towards the cupboard under the sink...and stopped. Turning, she said, "There's nane left."

"Too bad!" Wullie said, "Sorry pal it's a' done. Ah could gie ye a gless or two o' Scotland's other national drink if ye like?"

"And vot is zat?" the bomber asked with interest.

"It's called Dettol," Wullie said.

"Goot! I'll haff a glass of Dettol," the man said.

"Annie, wan gless o' Dettol for Fritz here," Wullie ordered.

"Nein, Nein," the German cried out.

"Ya greedy swine," Wullie snapped, "Wan gless isnae good enough for him.He wants bloody nine glesses."

"Nein, nein, my name iss not Fritz...it iss Hans."

Ina's eyesbrows shot up.

"Hans?" she cried, "We know a relative o' yours..int that funny? You come ower a' the wey frae Germany tae bomb us and wan o' yer ain relatives steys doon here."

"Whit ur you talkin' aboot?" Wullie snapped.

"Who iss zis relative off mine?" Hans asked quizically.

"FINGERS," Ina whooped, "Fingers McGeachie. You must be Hans McGeachie...in't that funny?"

Wullie threw Ina a contemptous glance.

"Don't talk bloody stupid," he said.

"Sorry, but I haff nein relatives here," Hans said.

"Oh, a whole squad o' ye, eh?" Ina said, "An' ye still come ower here for tae bomb us!"

"Ye don't look a bit like Fingers," Curdy McVey volunteered.

"Although any friend o' Fingers is a friend o' mine," he added.

"Shut yer face, Curdy,"Wullie snapped, "Or the next wake ye'll be goin' tae will be yer ain."

"Zat's ferry goot off you," Hans said, looking at Curdy, "perhaps you vood be goot enough to do me a small service?"

"Ah would be very pleased for to offer you ma professional services," Curdy said.

"Perhaps YOU could get me somsing to drink?"

"The only thing Ah can offer ye is some embalmin' fluid Ah've got which ye're welcome tae hiv."

"It vill get me drunk, ja?" the airman said with a wink.

"It'll get ye stiff, Ah can promise ye that," Curdy said.

"I vood also like somsing to eat," he went on. "YOU," he said,waving the gun towards Annie, "you get me somsing to eat."

"Ah've only got a wee bit o' cheese," Annie said worriedly.

"No salami?" Hans asked.

"Naw, he's a prisoner o' the Japs," Ina butted in.

"You should be ashamed o' yersel' comin' ower here and bombin' people," Annie said.

"I do it for ze Fatherland," Hans snapped, "I am an Aryan!"

"Ah'm no' interested in yer zodiac sign," Annie said.

"I am a staunch supporter of the Third Reich...and ve are vinning," Hans said with pride.

"Ah'm a staunch supporter o' the Third Lanark..and we're losin'," Wullie said despairingly.

"Under our glorious Fuehrer ve vill conquer ze vorld," Hans said, puffing his chest out.

"Away an' bile yer heid,"Wullie snapped. "Youse might have conquered the Norweigans, but ye'll never conquer the Glasweigans, Ah can tell ye that."

"Our glorious invasion forces vill be marchin' into Glasgow any day now, you vill see."

Rita gave a gasp and her hand came up to her mouth.

"Aw, naw!" she exclaimed, "an' me gettin' married, tae!"

Hans's eyebrows shot up.

"Ah, you are getting married sweet girl, eh?" he said.

"Aye, well Ah'm supposed tae..but your lot have spoilt things. Youse nearly sabotaged ma engagement when youse bombed McPhee's grocer's shoap and we had nae food for the party... Noo Ah hivnae got enough coupons for a weddin' dress and there's no' a bit of material anywhere in Glesca for a weddin' dress either. Ah hate youse!"

"I am sorry," Hans said, sounding genuinely contrite. "Look," he said, pulling a photograph out of his wallet, "Mein sister, Greta...she, too, is getting married...See."

Annie took the picture and looked at it closely.

"Aw, she's lovely!" she said, "The jackboots are nice tae. Is that Hitler that's staunin' beside her?"

"Nein, nein," Hans said, "Zat is my dear parent."

"Yer faither?" Annie asked.

"Mein mother," Hans said, replacing the photo in his wallet and tucking it safely inside his breast pocket.

"It widnae worry me," Ina said, "Ah'd walk doon the aisle even if Ah didnae have a weddin' dress."

"You'd walk doon wearin' a tottie sack," Wullie sniped, "and be just as shapely."

Ina ignored Wullie's sarcasm.

"Mein sister, Greta, she, too, is haffing problems finding a veddink dress," Hans volunteered, "But the ministry off Veddinks vill come to her aid. Ve haffa great system in our country."

"So great that youse a' want tae get oot and move intae other peoples' countries," Wullie snapped.

"Ve must expand, you see," Hans replied.

"If Goering expands any mair he'll explode," Wullie said, referring to the obese head of the Luftwaffe.

"Enough of zis," Hans snapped, "I must go to ze toilet, plees."

"Doon the stair, oan tha landin'," Annie said.

"Nein, nein, I cannot go down ze stairs and leaff you alone here...You vill try to get away. It iss too dangerous."

All eyes turned when a noise was heard coming from the lobby.

Rasputin, aroused from his slumber by the talking, entered, yawning and stretching, his Iron Cross, First Class, catching the light. Hans immediately jumped up.

"Mein Gott!" Hans cried, "the glorious invasion is here."

Hans hurried over and clasped Rasputin in a bear hug.

"Velcome, brother!" he cried, and, turning to the open-mouthed group, he said proudly, "Vot did I tell you, eh? Ve are here."

Thrusting the gun into Rasputin's hand, Hans cried; "Cover zem, vile I goes down to ze toilet."

Rasputin scratched his head.

"Grab him!" Wullie cried, "haud him Raspy."

Rasputin immediately took in the situation and stuck the gun up Hans' nose.

"You dirty rat," he said in his best James Cagney voice.

Wullie hurried over and took command. Taking the gun from Rasputin, in case it would go off, he snapped, "Right you, it's Tobago Street polis oaffice for you and then, nae doot, Maryhill Barracks. Ye'll get a good drink there, Ah'm sure."

"Lots of paraffin, ja?" Hans said, licking his lips in anticipation.

"Ja," Wullie said.

Wullie jabbed the gun into Hans' side and ordered him to march out in front of him.

"Just one zing, please," Hans pleaded.

"A'right, whit is it?" Wullie growled.

Hans made his way over to Rita and whispered into her ear. Rita smiled. Erchie immediately stepped in. His pride hurt, he held out his hand.

"Ah'll take that gun, Wullie," he snapped, "Ah am the official authority here."

"You're the wan that brought him up here," Wullie protested.

"It was him that brought ME up. He had a gun, don't forget," Erchie said. Wullie knew it was only right that Erchie should take Hans in. And Erchie saw a commendation coming his way...a great feather in his tin hat and a good lever for after the war when he hoped to join the regular Glasgow City Police force despite his small stature.

Wullie shrugged and handed over the gun.

Erchie pulled himself up to his full height.

"Right you...oot," he ordered. Hans shrugged and, turning to Rita, said, "I hope you haff a happy vedding. Auf Weidersehen...pet!"

A sharp jab of the gun pushed him out and through the door on to the stair landing.

Erchie marched Hans down the stairs and out into the street. His chest swollen with pride, he would march the German, gun wavering, up the full length of Well Street, past all the gaping faces at open windows, and on up to the swing park at the top of the street, and near to where the bomb had landed. That's where the blue police box stood. The Black Maria would arrive in no time and Erchie would be the toast of the Eastern Division. He saw himself snapping his heels, standing to rigid attention and saluting smartly as he stood before Mr. Percy Sillitoe, Glasgow's Chief Constable. Yes, he decided, life was good!

"Well, that's that!" Wullie said, flopping down on to the chair.

"Ah thought you were wonderful there, Wullie," Ina cooed. "They wey ye held that gun...ye were like Humphrey Bogart."

Wullie's chest went out three inches.

"Aye, well..er..nae German's gonny get the better o' me," Wullie said.

"Ah'm just goin' doon the stairs a minute, mammy," Rita said, hurrying out.

"Where are ye goin'?" Rasputin cried.

"Ah'll no' be long," Rita replied as she hurried down the stairs.

Curdy McVey yawned. The episode had sobered him up.

"Well, that'll be somethin' tae tell oor grandweans, eh?"

"Ah'll never have grandweans," Wullie growled.

"Ye never know yer luck," Ina said, fluttering her lashes.

Wullie was about to make a sarcastic reply when Rita, yelping with delight,came hurrying in.

"Oh look, mammy, just look at that," she cried, holding up the flowing white silk of a parachute.

"That's whit Hans whispered tae me when he was being led away. He said Ah reminded him o' his sister and that he'd hidden his parachute in the coarner o' the wash hoose…int that wonderful?" Rita, hugging the soft silk near to her cheek, danced around the table.

"It'll make a lovely weddin' dress, hen!" Annie said. "Who would have guessed that yer big day would be saved by a German who, earlier on, was tryin' tae kill ye?"

"Ah saw somethin' good in him right away," Ina piped up.

"You'd see somethin' good in Pontius Pilate," Wullie snapped.

"We'll get Mrs Cominsky tae work on that. She'll make a lovely joab o' it!" Annie said, a tear in her eye.

"Ah wish it was me," Ina said softly.

"You would need two bloody parachutes," Wullie said sarcastically.

"WULLIE!" Annie reproved.

"You shouldnae be lookin' at that," Ina said, turning to Rasputin.

"How no'?" he said, "it's just a bit o' cloth."

"It'll soon be a weddin' dress," Ina said.

Rasputin shrugged.

"No' before it's had a good wash," Annie said, gathering up the silk and putting it into the basket.

"Noo," she said, lifting up the basket of clothes, "where was Ah? Oh aye…"

Curdy and Rasputin hurried over and took the basket from her.

"Here," Curdy said, "We'll take that."

The trio made their way down to the back court and Curdy and Rasputin left Annie to get on with it.

Erchie had made a good job of stoking up the boiler and Annie put the clothes into the bubbling water. Everything had turned out well but she was disappointed. The Backcourt singer didn't arrive. There was to be no serenade. Annie sighed and, pulling the top away from the boiler, placed the dumpling in. THAT would be a treat for after the bells.

CHAPTER THREE

Curdy McVey bade farewell to Rasputin and headed for home. Wullie sat in deep thought thinking of all that happened. He smiled. He had quite enjoyed the adventure. He looked up. Rasputin was drooling over Rita. That was enough. He rose from the chair. He would go out and let the two lovebirds have some time alone together. After all, it had been more than six weeks since they had that privilege.

He made his way down to the street, turned left coming out of the close and headed on down towards Stevenston Street...and the Come Inn pub.

Some of the corner boys were standing around outside the Calton Social Club, which stood on the corner of Well Street and Stevenston Street and almost directly across the road from the pub. Wullie pushed his way through the swing doors. The pub was quiet and Jimmy Smith the barman was behind the bar cleaning glassses.

"It's yersel', Wullie," he said cheerily.

"Don't you talk tae me," Wullie snapped.

"Whit have AH done?" Jimmy asked sulkily.

"It's whit ye HIVNAE done," Wullie snapped, "A miserable hauf boattle on Hogmanay efter a' the custom Ah've gied you ower the years. Never wance hav Ah been sick on the flair..right?"

Jimmy nodded.

"Aye, right enough, ye always came in behind the counter."

"And not wance have Ah stood up on a table and sang 'The Sash', have Ah?" Wullie snorted.

"Ah...but there's a good reason for that, Wullie," Jimmy said.

"An' whit's THAT?" Wullie asked, knitting his brow.

"You're a catholic," Jimmy said.

"That's beside the point," Wullie snapped, "Ye'd think ye'd come and go seein' it's nearly Hogmanay...the greatest bevvy night o' the year."

"There's a war on, y'know, Wullie," Jimmy said, breathing on a glass and polishing it up with his apron.

"Aye, well, Ah'm no' gonny argue wi' ye nae mair. Ah'm in here tae see Fingers McGeachie. He's the only wan that helps anybody aroon' here."

"Did Ah hear ma hallowed name bein' mentioned there?" Fingers McGeachie said coming into the bar.

"Oh, it's yersel' Fingers", Willie said, turning.

"A hauf for Wullie, Jimmy," Fingers said, turning to the barman, "oot MA special boattle!"Jimmy poured a triple Scotch for Fingers and a small one for Wullie, who grunted and downed it in one small gulp.

"Right, Wullie," Fingers said, "we'll sit doon here and ye can gie's yer spiel." Fingers gave Jimmy a knowing wink and the barman poured two more.

"Cheers, old son," Fingers said, raising his glass. He smacked his lips. "Right, noo," he said, "whit's the problem? Don't tell me that pianna-teeth Rita's weddin' tae that big Idi..er..genius is aff? No' efter a' the trouble Ah went tae for acquirin' a deid pig for their last festivities."

Wullie shook his head.

"Naw, it's no' that, Fingers," he said. "They're gettin' married a'right. He'll be wearin' his German uniform and she'll be wearin' her parachute."

"Are they gettin married up in a balloon?" Fingers asked, puzzled.

"Naw, naw," Wullie said, "the only balloon at that weddin' will be the bridegroom. This meetin' between you and me has nothin' tae dae wi' Rita's weddin'. It is much mair important. It's aboot the greatest sacrilege that has ever happened."

"Don't tell me somebody's stole the poor boax oot o' St Alphonsus' chapel?" Fingers said.

"Naw, nothin' like that," Wullie said.

"The Freemasons hivnae bought it oot, have they?"

Wullie grimaced.

"This is no' a subject for lavatory, Fingers," he said, "it's serious!"

"Levity, Wullie," Fingers corrected the Malapropism,"levity, Noo gie's yer problem...spill it."

"That IS the problem, Fingers. There's no' much to spill this Hogmanay," Wullie moaned, "Ah've got wan hauf boattle for tae bring in the new year. Noo, you're a man who'll appreciate that this is not on."

Fingers threw up his arms.

"Och, is THAT yer problem?" he said

"Whit else?" Wullie said, "Ah mean, Ah've got ma reputation tae think aboot. Folk think Ah'm stoatin', so they dae."

"That's because they see ye stoatin' frae wan wa' tae the next," Fingers said. "It's a different kind o' stoatin', Wullie. But have nae fear Fingers is here." Fingers breathed on his fingernails and polished them on the lapel of his expensive gaberdine suit.

"Ye..ye mean ye've got a source, Fingers?" Wullie said in awe.

"Have ah got a source, or have Ah got a source?" Fingers repeated. It wasn't a question. And Wullie was truly hooked. Was there nothing this man couldn't produce?

"Have Ah got a source?" Fingers repeated, tapping the side of his nose with his forefinger.

"Drink up! Wullie," he said, "For Ah am gonny show you somethin' that'll make yer eyes pop." Wullie downed his drink in one quick gulp.

He knew he could rely on Fingers. They had grown up together and, although Wullie was a few years older, he felt that Fingers McGeachie was always there, somewhere in his life, ever since they played on the dusty asphalt of Well Street.

"Ye know, Fingers," Wullie said, recalling those happy days of the past. "Ah was just thinkin' how well you've done for yersel'...gettin' a hoose up a wally close, gaberdine suits...like that..." Fingers's chest swelled.

"Aye, well, it's a metter of survival, Wullie," he said, "Ah appreciate whit Ah've got. As ye say, it's nice tae have nice things. This gaberdine suit, which you have obviously appreciated, is the real thing...tailor made from the cloth of a real gaber. Ah don't like anything that's no' real."

"Ah was just lookin' back, Fingers," Wullie said. "Remember how we used tae play that gemme called efter a Jewish man?"

"Whit gemme was that, Wullie?" Fingers said, knitting his brows.

"That gemme where ye had three holes in a straight line in the grun', separated a yard apart. Then we'd throw in pennies...you know..that Jewish gemme."

"Jewish?" Fingers asked, puzzled.

"Aye, it was a gemme wi the title of a Jewish man."

"Whit was it called?" Fingers asked

"MOSHIE," Wullie cried. "How could ye forget that, Fingers? You were the best player in the street and used tae leave the rest o' us staunin' wi' bare pockets."

"Och, aye, Ah remember noo!" Fingers said, although he had never connected the popular game with the name of any Jewish gentleman.

Wullie was now on a pure nostalgic flight.

"Then we had hudgies...remember that?" Wullie said.

"Oh, aye,"Fingers laughed. "That's where we held on tae the hoarse and cert for a free hurl, right?"

"Aye," Wullie said, "that's right. Even playin' at that you had yer ain rules, Fingers. Ye were supposed tae hing oan the back o' the cert...no' on the front wi' yer airms roon' the hoarse's neck."

"Aye, they were the days, Wullie, they were the days!" Fingers smiled.

"Even yer weddin' was different," Wullie recalled. "In the Windsor Restuarant, at Brigton Cross, wisn't it?"

"Aye, that's right," Fingers replied.

"Aye, Ah mind it fine!" Wullie said, "Ah remember goin' into the hall and a' the balloons were on the flair, and ye dropped the dancers frae the ceilin'...."That was definitely an innovation, Fingers!"

"Aye, well Ah was just tryin' tae put some novelty intae things, know whit Ah mean?" Fingers laughed.

"It was just a shame yer marriage didnae work oot, Fingers," Wullie said sadly.

"Aye, well that's life, Wullie," Fingers said, "Ah mean, when Ah saw ma Sadie constantly goin' up that close at number twenty-four, Ah thought she was puttin' oan a line wi' Wee Hector, the bookie. Instead o' that she was daein' a bloody line wi' Wee Hector. Well, that was that!"

"Aye, sad, very sad," Wullie said.

He was brought back to earth by a strong slap on the back.

"Hey, "Fingers cried, "let's get oot o' this depression. C'mon, Wullie, Ah've got somethin' tae show ye."

Fingers got up from the table and Wullie followed.

"See ye, Jimmy," Fingers said with a wave to Jimmy Smith, who was still cleaning glasses. Jimmy nodded.

""Aye, Ah hope yer cellar gets flooded," Wullie said in passing.

"An' Ah hope your bladder bursts," Jimmy replied.

Fingers put an arm around Wullie's shoulder and steered him towards Claythorn Steet. Wullie McSorley's chest puffed out. Yes, he was a happy man being a confidant and friend of the great Fingers McGeachie.

It was mid-afternoon. The old year was drawing to a close. Rita and Rasputin had decided to pay a visit to Barrowland Ballroom in the evening but would make sure to be home in time for 'a good night's rest'.

Rasputin, traumatised by his encounter with the German pilot and the fact that he had held a 'real' gun in his hand, had, once more, retired to the room and lain down.

Rita was glancing through The Bulletin when she let out a cry.

"Oh, mammy..look, Treron's have a sale on. Och, Ah wish Ah had some money! Ah could've maybe got some wee accessories..know whit Ah mean...for ma weddin'. Ah'm goin' intae toon anywey, tae get the licence an' that and Ina says she'll come wi' me."

Annie said nothing. She went to the sideboard drawer, took out a slip of green paper and handed it to Rita, who was still reading the morning paper.

"Whit's this?" Rita asked.

"It's for you, hen," Annie said, "Ah got it for just this kind of occasion."

"A Provident Cheque!" Rita screamed, "for FIVE POUNDS! Aw, mammy, you're a darlin', so ye are." Rita threw her arms round Annie's neck and kissed her heavily on the cheek.

Annie flushed with embarrassment.

Annie often got a Provident Cheque. She found them a Godsend when money was scarce. They were given out by credit companies and were usually used for purchasing clothing...although some people would receive them and immediately sell the cheque for a few pounds lower value so as to get ready cash.

"Aye, well Ah know whit like it is," she said. "When yer faither and me were gettin' married, yer granny gave him a Bristol Cheque for two pounds and ten shullins. Noo, he could've went oot and drank that but he didnae. His first thoughts were of me. He wanted me tae have a smile on ma face on oor weddin' day so he went right oot and bought me a new set o' teeth."

"Aye, ma' da has always been considerate!" Rita said.

A loud rap on the door made them look up. Ina McLatchie breezed in, pulling on her gloves.

"Right, are ye ready, hen?" she said.

"Just tae get ma coat, Ina," Rita said, lifting her coat from the hook on the door.

"We'll no' be long, mammy," she said. "C'mon, Ina."

"First stop Martha Street Registry Oaffice," Ina said as they hurried down the stairs. "Got yer hauf croon ready for yer licence?"

"Oh aye, "Rita said, "Raspy's no' gonny get away for the sake o' a hauf croon."

The girls laughed as they turned right, up towards London Road where they got on a green number eighteen 'caur' heading towards the town and Springburn.

They sat upstairs and chatted until the tram reached Lewis' Polytechnic, 'The Polly', in Argyle Street, where they alighted and walked up Mitchell Street, across George Square and on, up into Cathedral Street and finally Martha Street.

Ina shivered as they entered the building.

"Ye know," she said, "it gies me a funny feelin' bein' in here, so it does. It disnae seem that long since Ah was in here wi' yer mammy registerin' ma da's death."

"Ah know how ye feel, Ina," Rita said, giving her arm a comforting squeeze.

The wee man behind the desk peered over the top of his pince-nez and coughed weakly.

"Is your fiancée in the armed forces?" he inquired.

"Oh, aye," Rita enthused. "He is advisor tae General Montgomery."

"Oh, aye!" the wee man said, peering closer with dubiety.

"We would like to get married as soon as possible," Rita went on, "in case he has suddenly to go to Germany on a secret mission..for to shoot Hitler or somebody."

"Oh aye!" the man said. "Noo,is yer man-to- be local?"

"Oh naw!" Rita cried, "He's a genius. There's nothin' loco aboot HIM!"

"Naw, naw," the wee man said, "Ah meant is he LOCAL? Is he frae Glesca..or Scotland..or Britain...know whit Ah mean?"

Rita nodded, "Of definitely!" she exclaimed, "He is Glesca born an' bred."

The wee man dipped his pen into the the inkwell.

"And whit is said fiancé's name?"

"Rasputin," Rita said, almost with reverence.

The wee man spluttered.

"Rasputin?" he said, drawing his heavy eyebrows together.

"He was called efter a monk," Rita said, "His maw was very religious."

"Was his faither a Russian?" the man asked.

"Ivan? Naw, Ah don't think so. That's a Welsh name, intit...Ivan?"

"Ivan the Terrible!" the wee man muttered.

"Aw naw, Ah widnae say that!" Rita said "He took a drink, right enough and belted Raspy's maw, Mischka, noo and again. But Ah widnae say he was terrible."

The clerk continued to fill up the forms, finally putting the last dot on with a flourish.

"Voila!" he said, "Now that'll be hauf a croon, please." Rita gave him the coin and held the paper to her breast.

"Cheap at hauf the price!" she muttered."Ah feel Raspy's really mine, noo," she laughed.

"Ah wish it was me that was gettin' wan," Ina said as they stepped into the street.

"Ach, never mind," Rita softly said, "your turn'll come, Ina. Uncle Wullie will get the message wan o' these days."

The two girls walked along Cathedral Street and into Bath Street past the headquarters of the Glasgow Corporation Transport Department which was heavily sandbagged.

They turned into Renfield Street, crossed the road, passing the Queen Anne Restaurant, and turned into Sauchiehall Street. Treron's store was doing brisk business and Rita took her time going round the various departments. Most of the goods required clothing coupons but others did not and Rita purchased a patent leather black handbag and some toilet accessories.

The sun was still shining as they stepped out into the street. All along the avenue of shops were sandbagged. Some of the shop windows were boarded up with only slats for the window shopper to peer through.

The girls turned west, along towards Charing Cross. They got some wolf whistles as they passed by the large, imposing building of the Beresford Hotel, now under the occupation of the American Army.

Polish and Canadian and Free French servicemen, too, gave them a wink and and a whistle and, while it rubbed off Rita, Ina tingled and enjoyed the flattery.

"We'll have a cup o' tea in Miss Buick's Tearoom," Rita said, turning into the popular venue. They were lucky. One table only was available. The smart waitress took their order and was back in minutes with a silver teapot of steaming hot tea and a plate of newly baked muffins.

"Ah suppose Ah'll need tae go doon tae St Alphonsus' and see the priest aboot the banns an' that!" Rita exclaimed.

"Oh, aye!" Ina said, "That is very important...although Ah think they come and go a lot because some o' the men only have short leaves and might be sent abroad an' that...know whit Ah mean?"

Rita nodded. Thank heaven Rasputin was now in the forces. Things would get speeded up, she thought to herself.

"We could walk," Ina said.

Rita and Ina made their way down Hope Street and into Argyle Street. They walked on, through the Trongate, past Glasgow Cross and on up London Road and past 'The Barras'. St Alphonsus's stood near the 'Barras', the outdoor market, at the top of Kent Street. They rang the highly polished brass bell of the Chapel House, in Stevenston Street. The elderly housekeeper showed them into a sitting room which smelt of chintz and furniture polish. A huge mahogany table sat in the middle of the floor and two large green upholstered easy chairs sat at each end of a low grate in which a fire crackled. Ina warmed her hands and Rita felt a little nervous. Minutes later they were joined by Father Hourigan, the parish Priest. Father Hourigan was a rotund, portly gentleman with a deep, gruff voice which frightened some people.

"Good afternoon ladies," he said cheerily and sat on a dining chair at the table. "And what can I do for you?"

"Ah want tae get married here," Rita said

"You're one of my parishioners?" the good priest inquired.

"Oh aye," Rita said, "Ah even go tae confession when Ah don't need tae go tae confession."

"What about your husband-to-be?" Father Hourigan asked.

"He's no' of this parish, Father" Rita said.

"He's no' of this planet either," Ina said.

Father Hourigan's brows shot up.

"He IS of the faith, though?"

"Oh aye, Father," Rita said, "he's called efter a monk."

"Oh!" Father Hourigan said, "Who? St Benedict? St. Francis? St Enoch?"

"Aw, Father, 'ye're a real joker," Rita laughed and had to stop herself from jabbing him the ribs with her elbow. "Whit mother would call her wean efter a railway station?"

"Well, who IS he named after?" Father Hourigan asked, hiding a smile.

"Rasputin," Rita said.

"Oh, is he orthodox?" Father Hourigan asked.

"Aw, Father, you are a one," Rita cried, "Ah can definitely say that he's pretty normal."

"No, no," the priest said, "With a name like Rasputin, I thought he might be Russian."

"Naw, naw, He's frae Govan originally. He's a Governor."

"Right," Father Hourigan said, " I'll attend to things. He's in the services?"

"The army, Father, the Pioneer Corps. He's advisor tae General Montgomery."

"Aye well all Rasputins were advisors to the nobility," the priest said.

"Did ye hear that Ina?" Rita clapped her hands, "Good Auld Raspy is just daein' whit comes naturally!"

"Right, then," Father Hourigan said, "I'll get things moving."

Rita hesitated. "Er...would it be a'right if Ah wear a parachute for ma weddin'?" she said.

"Ye can wear a barrage balloon if ye like," Father Hourigan said.

"But it's a GERMAN parachute, Father," Rita said.

"Just as long as it hisnae got swastikas on it, the priest said,"that's no' the kind o' cross Ah want in MA chapel."

Rita left the chapel house elated.

"He was awfu' nice, wisn't he?" she said to Ina.

"Ah only wish he would mairry ME!" Ina said.

"Priests canny get married, Ina," Rita reminded her.

"Ah meant Me and Wullie," Ina said dreamily.

"Ye'd like Father Hourigan tae conduct the weddin' ceremony?" Rita said.

"Ah'd let Charlie Chaplin conduct ma weddin' ceremony," Ina said. "But Father Hourigan was awfu' nice at ma da's funeral. And when he heard ma da' inspired Walt Disney tae create Goofy, he was a' ower me, so he was!"

Rita and Ina turned into Kent Street and then London Road. They could have walked the few hundred yards back to Well Street by just going along Stevenston Street, where St Alphonsus' chapel house was. But they would not have passed Margaret Forrester's shop and Rita wanted to have another look in that window.

The flowing wedding dress was still there. But suddenly it didn't really matter any more. Mrs Cominsky was already at work on the parachute on her treadled old Singers sewing machine in her 'single-end' up the Paddy close. And, as far as Rita was concerned, her mother had convinced her that Mrs Cominsky, of patchwork quilt fame, could take on any of the Paris designers.

Rita smiled. Everything was going her way. Rita and Ina stopped at Mario Valente's chip shop. The big Italian still had the notice in his window proclaiming: "I have two sons in the British Army...Long Live Scotland!"

"Ah, ma wee-a Rio Rita!" he cried, "And yer Auntie Bella, eh?"

"Naw, that's Ina McLatchie...no' ma Auntie Bella," Rita laughed.

"Well it-a disnae- a matter," Mario said, "You no'-workin' the day, eh? No' oan-a the caurs, eh?"

"Naw, no' the day, Mario," Rita said, "We were away at the registry oaffice gettin' ma licence for tae get merried."

"Big-Raspitin' is hame, eh? No' away fightin' the Germans?"

"Naw, he's hame for tae bring in the bells the morra night. It'll be Hogmanay, Mario."

"Och, Ah know-a that!" Mario laughed, "We're gettin' a' prepared for to bring in the new-a year. The current bun and thee-a shorat-a- bried...no'a forgettin' the ginger wine."

"Aye, we'll hope the war'll finish next year, Mario, and then we can a' live in peace?" Rita said.

"Aye, that's-a right," Mario said wistfully, "Then maybe Ah can-a get a wee-a visit hame to Milano and see ma- auld- maw." Tears were not far away from the big man's dark eyes.

"Anyway," he said, cheering up, "You're-a gettin' spliced, eh? Ah wish Ah was-a twenty years-a younger, ah'dve been efter ye-a masel'...if Mrs-a Valente would've let me, eh?" Mario's stomach wobbled as he laughed loudly.

"It widnae worry me whit age a man was," Ina said, "ah'd mairry him even if he was a hunner an' forty!"

""Naw, naw, get somebody yer ain-age," Mario said, "aboot-a sixty-four."

"Here! Ah'll let you know that Ah'm just in ma late forties," Ina cried.

"Trust-a me tae put-a ma foot in it," Mario said, "Oh, and talkin' aboota foots, are ye still-a gettin' yer custard baths, ma wee-a Rita?"

"MUSTARD, Mario!" Rita corrected, "it's a MUSTARD bath Ah plank ma feet in efter staunin' on that caur a' day."

"Aye, ye're a good-a lassie and a hard-a worker," Mario said, "And ye're ma favourite customer. Noo, here's two fish suppers for ye...wi' a wee bit extra fish for you and yer Auntie Bella."

"Ah am NOT her Auntie Bella!" Ina cried, "But Ah hope wan day that we WILL be related."

"Aye, well, a happy new years tae you when it comes. And here's hopin' ye find a young-a man tae share your affections, Bella!"

"Even an AULD man, Mario," Ina laughed. "Anythin' up tae a hundred."

Mario laughed loudly along with Ina...but her laugh was hollow.

Ina and Rita hurried on towards Well Street. Rita wanted time to prepare for her night out at Barrowland. But she had more urgent plans to put into action first. She would pick up Rasputin and both of them would go on their very important search.

Wee Hughie Dunn sat behind the bar in the Calton Social Club when Rasputin and Rita entered. The punters hadn't yet arrived for the night's dancing. Hughie stood up and extended his hand.

"Welcome to the Calton Social Club, hen!" he said, "And whit can Ah dae for youse?"

"We're gettin' married in a few weeks," Rita said, "And we were wonderin' if we could haud oor reception in here?"

"It's good staggerin' distance frae Rita's hoose, y'see," Rasputin said.

"We WERE gonny go tae the Windsor Restaurant, at Brigton Croass, but ma mammy says that we should keep oor money locally wi' oor ain people," Rita added.

Wee Hughie stood up and stretched his full four-foot eleven.

"THAT is very patriotic!" he said. "Ur you not the daughter of Big Sammy, at present the guest of Her Majesty's enemies?"

"Ah am," Rita said, "Ma daddy is noo wi' the Japs."

"Did he get fed up bein' wi' the Germans?" Hughie asked.

"He tried tae escape frae the Germans an' took a wrang turn," Rita sighed.

"Aye, Ah could believe that," Hughie said, "He did a few turns here and was bloody hopeless. Is this the man ye're gonny mairry?"

Rita nodded and gave Rasputin's arm an affectionate squeeze.

"It is." she said, "He is ma dream man."

"If ye ask me," Hughie said, "Ah think ye've been hivin' nightmares. If ye don't mind me sayin' so. Ah think ye could dae better than that!"

"Whit does that mean?" Rita said angrily.

"Well, look at him," Hughie said, screwing up his nose, "He's like wan o' the Broons."

"Aye, he does have that intelligent look," Rita said. "Ye think he looks like Hen Broon?"

"Mair like Daphne Broon," Hughie said.

"Ah'll let you know that Ah'm a genius," Rasputin said. "Ah was only three years auld when Ah invented false teeth."

"False teeth hiv been around for years," Hughie snapped.

"No, musical wans!" Rasputin answered. Hughie raised his eyebrows. "Musical wans?" he said.

"Aye," Rasputin said, puffing out his chest.

"Whit good are they?" Hughie sneered.

"They were a great help tae folk that wur shy," Rasputin said. "For instance, somebody at a party who was too shy for tae sing when asked. A' they had tae dae was staun up and show their teeth an' no' only were they smilin' at the crowd, suddenly they filled the hoose wi' music. Ma maw loved hers … she was shy, y'see and, tae hide her shyness, she got stuck intae the gin."

"And her musical teeth helped her?" Hughie said, knitting his eyebrows.

"Oh aye," Rasputin said, "She used tae just walk intae the pub, stroll up tae the bar, smile at the barman and oot would come 'A Gordon For Me.'"

"Ah see!" Hughie said sceptically.

"Only trouble was they kept ma da' awake a' night," Rasputin added, "Ma maw kept them in a gless o' watter at her bedside and a' night it was like listenin' tae an underwatter concert."

"Aye, well Ah'm afraid oor hall is booked for the foreseeable future," Hughie said. "Oor baun' has been called up. We could, of course, always hire yer maw's teeth but Ah think yer guests would get fed up a' night just dancin' tae the Gay Gordons. Try the Brigton Public Hall."

Rasputin and Rita left hand in hand and downcast. The Calton Social Club was handy … just down at the foot of Well Street and facing the Come Inn pub.

They hurried up the street and on to London Road just as a number twenty-six red car going to Burnside was screeching to a stop.

Wee Peggy McAlpine, the conductress, smiled at Rita and gave her a knowing wink. The fares were waived aside. Wee Peggy ran a menage at the Ruby Street tram depot and had often helped Rita out of a financial crisis.

Rasputin and Rita alighted at Bridgeton Cross and hurried along the few hundred yards up London Road to the red-bricked public halls.

Big Malky, the caretaker, licked his fingers and thumbed through the book.

"Gettin' married, eh?" he said, "Youse have left it a bit late!"

"Ah am nut pregnant!" Rita snapped. "Ah've put on a wee bit weight right enough," she added.

"Naw, naw, hen," Big Malky said, "Ah meant youse are a bit late bookin' yer hall. We seem tae be filled up for months. Let's see, noo…?" he went on, perusing the book.

"Noo, there's a barmitsvah for wee Sean O'Reilly. Then there's a British Film Night where they show British Films … that's for the Brigton

Masochist Society. Then we've got a concert starring a wee wuman playing her musical teeth ... her speciality being "Smiling Through". Naw, sorry, we ur full up. Ye'll either have tae forget yer weddin' or have a clabber."

"We'll try the Windsor Restaurant!" Rita said, tugging at Rasputin's sleeve.

The Windsor Restaurant, at Bridgeton Cross, was fully booked and the manageress showed the young couple sympathy and suggested a small community hall, in Salamanca Street, off Duke Street, where, she heard, a friend's daughter held a very successful wedding reception.

Plooky Boyle ran his finger down the pages of the large book and stopped suddenly with a whoop of delight.

"Youse are in luck!" he pronounced, "It jist so happens we have a spare night on January 22nd. It WIS booked for Auld Maggie Broon's 104th Birthday celebrations but, alas, she'll no' be around for it!" Plooky stared somberly at the ground.

"Poor auld sowel!" Rita said, "when did she snuff it?"

"Oh, she's no' deid," Plooky said, "She eloped wi' a shullin' a weak man."

"Ooooh!" Rita exclaimed.

"Noo," Plooky went on, "Ah can supply the baun' for yer weddin' if youse like."

"Well," Rasputin said, "We were gonny try and save money and jist hire ma maw."

"Oh, does yer maw play the accordion or somethin'?" Plooky asked, raising his brows.

"Naw, her teeth," Rasputin said.

"Ah shouldnae hiv asked," Plooky said.

"Naw, Ah think we SHOULD get a baun'! Rita said. "We canny have your maw a' dressed up at the reception and expect her for tae staun' up and play her teeth. Ah mean, she gets carried away when she plays a flamenco and has tae take them oot for her castanets effect."

"Right then," Plooky said, "Whit colour o' baun' would youse like?"

"Ye mean ye've got bauns o' different colours?" Rasputin said screwing his nose. "Ah suppose black musicians are great at jazz, right enough."

"Naw, we've nae BLACK bauns," Plooky said shaking his head. "We've jist got two colours ..."

"Whit's that?" Rasputin said.

"Orange or green," Plooky said.

"Whit's the difference?" Rasputin asked.

"Well," Plooky explained, "the orange baun' has got a flute section."

"And the green?" Rita asked, narrowing her eyes.

"They've got a Guinness section. The mair blootered they get, the better they play," Plooky grinned.

"We'll think aboot it," Rita said.

"We can also supply a three-tiered cake … withoot food coupons, if youse know whit Ah mean," Plooky said, tapping the side of his nose.

"Oh, that would be a help!" Rita whooped. "How can ye manage that?"

"It's a' thanks tae Wee Scruffy Duffy," Plooky said. "He is a master baker and has discovered a wey for tae make weddin' cakes wi' a marzipan substitute that he has invented. He is brilliant, so he is!"

"Whit's the substitute?" Rita asked narrowing her eyes once more.

"It's ingenius," Plooky said, "it's basis is sawdust mixed wi' a secret ingredient that Scruffy discovered."

"Has Scruffy baked wan before?" Rita asked.

"Oh aye!" Plooky said, "He baked wan for Mrs Lane's daughter, Lisa's weddin'. It looked beautiful!"

"Whit did it taste like?" Rita asked, now showing interest.

"Like eatin' a plank," Plooky said.

Rita glanced at Rasputin who shook his head.

"Ah don't think we'll bother, Rita," he said, "It sounds like a cake where ye widnae need a knife tae cut it. Ye would need a saw."

"Aye, jist forget the cake, Mr Plooky," Rita said. "And we'll let ye know aboot the baun'."

The happy couple left the hall and walked up towards Parkhead Cross where they would catch a car going down Gallowgate.

"Are you sure ye'll get leave on the 22nd o' January, Raspy?" Rita asked, squeezing his hand.

"Och, aye!" Rasputin said, "Ah'll have a word wi' Monty and ask him for tae postpone any elephant attack till Ah get back."

"He must be a very kind man!" Rita sighed.

"Oh, he is!" Rasputin said, "When he kicked me oot his oaffice, he took aff his big heavy boots and put oan his slippers."

Rasputin puffed out his chest. He had the air of a man who had command of the ear of one of Britain's greatest generals.

Rasputin and Rita alighted from the tram at Bain Square and cut through to London Road where they popped into Peter Rossi's cafe and ordered a McCallum to celebrate their acquiring a hall for their wedding reception.

Annie was delighted that Rita and Rasputin had managed to get fixed up with the hall.

"When yer faither an' me got married," she said to Rita, "we tried tae hire a Masonic hall for the reception but yer da' ended up in the Royal Infirmary."

"Whit happened, mammy?" Rita asked worriedly.

"Yer faither went intae St Alphonsus' chapel hall by mistake an' gied the caretaker the auld haun' shake and got chucked oot the windae."

"So, whit did youse dae?" Rasputin asked.

"Chinged oor religion," Annie said, "we knew we'd need that hall for other occasions … like your Christenin' for instance … which wisnae faur off."

"Ach ye did well anywey, mammy," Rita said, putting an affectionate arm around her mother's shoulder.

Annie sighed.

"Aye, things were hard then!" she said, "Yer faither was oot o' work and ended up goin' roon the backcourts singin' …"

"Whit a shame!" Rita said.

"But it was through that he got a joab … A coalman who was aff work wi' a sore throat signed him up right away."

"So, some good came oot o' it mammy!" Rita smiled.

"Oh aye!" Annie said, "it was better than walkin' the streets."

"It must take a loat of heart tae go roon' the backcourts singin'," Rasputin said.

"As faur as Sammy was concerned," Annie said, "it took a loat o' gall. It was his nose y'see. He had a some size o' a conk and was plagued wi' sinus trouble a' the time."

"He had a big nose?" Rasputin queried, raising his eyebrows.

"Big nose?" Annie said, "Wan Friday efternin he was staunin' ootside the close and he blew his nose and Martin's Leather Works shut doon for the weekend!"

"Ah don't believe that, Mammy," Rita said.

"Believe it if ye like, hen," Annie said, "but when we were staunin' in the hoose and he kissed me, we had tae open the windae."

Rasputin laughed loudly when Wullie entered.

"Whit's a the laughter?" Wullie enquired.

"Ah was just sayin' that ma Sammy had a big nose," Annie chuckled.

Wullie laughed.

"Ah widnae say it was big, but they called him the '*elephant man*".

"Talkin' aboot elephants," Rasputin said, "Monty thought that my idea o' usin' them would take the Germans by surprise. That they'd throw doon their erms and throw up their erms."

"Aye, Ah can seen them throwin' up their erms," Wullie said, "and convulsin' wi' laughter."

Rasputin was hurt.

"Hannibal used them," he said.

"Noo Screwball wants tae use them," Wullie said.

"Noo, we wull have nae mair talk o' elephants," Annie said. "There is mair important things tae discuss."

"Like whit?" Wullie snapped.

"Like me gettin' a baun' for ma weddin'," Rita said.

Rita had thought of approaching Billy MacGregor whose band packed them in at the Barrowland Ballroom but had decided if the reception was going to be in the small Salamanca Street hall, there would be no room for the guests.

Her thoughts were shattered by the sudden wailing of the air-raid warning.

"Right, c'mon," Annie said, taking command. "Doon tae the dunny and Wullie, leave they wally dugs on the mantlepiece. They'll be quite safe and the mice are frightened tae come oot because o' their presence."

Ina came running in, hand at her mouth in panic.

"Oh Wullie," she cried grabbing his arm, "whit if it's parachutists they're drappin'?"

"You'll no need for tae worry," Wullie said with irritation, "wan look at you an' they'll think we've got a secret weapon."

The mouth organ player was playing 'Blue Birds Over the White Cliffs of Dover' as they entered the shelter up the pend. Some people were already there and singing half-heartedly.

"Oh, no' that bloody mouth organ man again!" Wullie said despairingly.

"Aye, ye get fed up listenin' tae that mooth organ," Rasputin said, "Even ma maw's teeth would be a chinge."

The sing-song continued with renditions of 'Run Rabbit Run' and 'Mairzy Doats an' Dozy Doats' following.

Wullie sat holding his ear taking his hands away only now and again to slap Ina's wandering paws.

Wullie had decided that Jerry would come over this night … despite its closeness to Hogmanay – he was sure that this would be just the first wave. There would be, he reckoned a second wave. Hitler was not going to miss the opportunity of demoralising Glaswegians as they geared up for the big night.

The singing went on for more than an hour and, with great relief, Wullie heard the 'All Clear'. Ina continued to hang on to his arm as they left the shelter and hurried across the street to number twenty-seven.

Wullie had been overawed at the quality of the wally tiles on the walls of Finger's close.

"Aw, they're really somethin', Fingers," he said. "Ah have never seen such a clean wa'! It's every bit as nice as the Gents' lavvy in St Vincent Street."

"Aye, a wipe doon wi' vinegar does wonders, "Fingers said, "no' only dae ye have a dazzlin' wa', but it smells like a chip shoap."

Fingers, his arm around Wullie's shoulder, steered him up the stairs.

"Noo, Wullie," Fingers said, "Whit you are about for to see is strictly secret … understaun'?"

Wullie nodded. "Ah am the ephiphany of silence," he said.

"Have ye ever heard of an illicit still, Wullie?" Fingers said in a whisper.

"Ye mean somethin' like a nude photay o' Rita Hayworth?" Wullie gasped, his jaw open.

"Naw, naw," Fingers said with irritation, "An illicit still … ye know whit Moonshine is, don't ye."

"Aye, like sunshine at night," Wullie said.

"Have ye ever heard o' the HillBillies?" Fingers asked.

"Aye, of coorse, Ah have, "Wullie said, a little hurt, "That's they orange-men that live up Cathkin Braes."

Fingers was in despair.

"Wullie," he said, "Ye've surely heard of BOOTLEGGIN', hiven't ye? "Well, that's ma latest business enterprise. Ah am goin' intae competition wi' the big boys."

"That's marvellous!" Wullie exclaimed, "Ye're takin' on Saxone and Easiphit an' that? Ah didnae know ye were intae shoes an' that, Fingers."

"It's got nothin' tae dae wi' shoes, Wullie," Fingers snapped. "It's the dis-tillers Ah am takin' on … Ah read this book, 'How for tae make yer own Bevvy', by a wee Italian called Al Capone."

"Is that the wee bloke who's got a chip shoap in Govan Road?" Wullie asked innocently.

"He's frae Chicago, Wullie," Fingers said." A long wey away!"

"It is if ye're desperate for a fish supper," Wullie said.

"This wey, "Fingers said as they entered the flat. Fingers led Wullie to the bathroom and, with a flourish, threw open the door.

"Voila!" he said and stepped back to allow Wullie to take in fully the scene before him. There was a Heath Robinson contraption with copper pipes and bottles and large glass containers. A huge white bath stood against the wall, half full of brown liquid which splashed against its sides.

Wullie's jaw dropped!

"Is that bath where ye keep yer booze, Fingers?" he asked.

"Aye," Fingers said proudly, "that's it."

Wullie immediately turned on him. Pointing to the bathtub, he cried, "That, Fingers, is sacrilege, so it is. Using a beautiful white enamelled bath for the purpose of keepin' hame-made liquor in. That is a mortal sin, Fingers. That bath was put there for wan purpose and wan purpose only … for tae haud coal!"

"Well, ye've got tae use yer initiative, Wullie," Fingers said. "Ye must use whit ye've got. Here, look, Ah'm gonny present you wi' a couple o' boatles of ma special booze, Wullie."

Wullie took the two bottles offered and held them up to the light.

"They look a'right!" he remarked.

"Of coorse they're a'right, Wullie," Fingers said proudly. "There's just wan thing. If ye don't like the taste, it's very good as a paint stripper."

"Whit particular brand o'booze have ye got?" Wullie asked with interest.

"Whisky, vodka, brandy, creme de menthe, gin … but there's just wan thing …!"

"Whit's that?" Wullie asked.

"It a' tastes the same," Fingers said.

"Whit does it a' taste like, then?" Wullie wanted to know, "Whisky, Gin … or whit?"

"Turpentine," Fingers said.

"WHIT?" Wullie cried out.

Fingers laughed loudly.

"Only kiddin', Wullie he said, "Only kiddin'."

"That's great, makin' a' they varieties, so it is," Wullie said in awe. "Are ye makin' much?"

"Ah'm turnin' it oot by the gallon, Wullie. By the gallon," Fingers repeated.

"Ah've heard o' a Fingers' Stall," Wullie laughed, "But never a Finger's Still." Fingers guffawed at Wullie's weak joke.

Wullie lifted a cup and, with one sweep down the bath, filled it. He took a good swig and, grimacing, spat it out.

"Geez!" he cried, "That tastes like bath watter!"

Taking the cup from him, Fingers said, "It IS bath watter, Ah had a bath before Ah went oot."

"Yeuch!" Wullie exclaimed. Fingers took a bottle and filled it.

"Here," he said, try that."

Wullie downed the contents in one gulp. Smacking his lips, he said, "THAT, Fingers, was marvellous. Ah just canny make up ma mind whit it was … whisky, gin, or whit. Naw, Ah couldnae tell ye. Ah gie in. Whit was it?"

"Iron Brew," Fingers said, "Ah lifted the wrang boattle!"

"Let's try this," Wullie said, placing his cup under one of the copper pipes. He filled the cup and knocked it back in a oner. Smacking his lips, he said, "Aw, that was pure nectar, Fingers, pure nectar."

"Ah'm gled ye think so," Fingers said.

"Aye, it's somethin' Ah've never tasted before, Fingers," Wullie said, "Whit dae ye call it?"

"Watter, Wullie," Fingers said, "the booze hisnae come through the pipes yet."

Wullie shook his head and smiled. Looking around Fingers' flat he had to admit that the 'Big Man' was in a class of his own.

The place was packed with the most exquisite stuff Wullie had ever clapped eyes on.

"Aw, ye've done really well for yersel', Fingers," Wullie said in awe. "Ye've got stuff here Ah've never, ever seen before anywhere. Look at a' the pictures on the wa'!! They ur REALLY somethin!"

"They're a' originals that were en route tae the Art Galleries … but … er … fell aff the back o' a lorry," Fingers gave a discreet cough.

"Geez! There's no' a mark on them, either." Wullie remarked.

"This yin," Fingers said, indicating a large painting," is by Whistler … the great dug trainer. And this wan is by Constable, who painted these wonderful pictures before goin' out on his beat."

"Who painted that ugly auld swine, Fingers?" Wullie asked, showing interest in Fingers' commentary.

"That's a mirror, Wullie," Fingers said.

"Ye've got beautiful stuff, Fingers."

"Ah frequent Paddy's Market," Fingers said.

Wullie's eyes swept the room.

"That's a lovely big accordion in the coarner, Fingers. Ah'll bet that cost ye a few bob, eh?"

"That's a grand pianna, Wullie," Fingers said. "It wance graced the orchestra pit in the Queens Theatre, in Watson Street."

"Aw, Ah love the Queens," Wullie said, "Frank and Doris Dory, Sammy Murray and no' forgettin' Glesca's very best Principal Boy ... Ivy Val."

"Aye, a great theatre!" Fingers agreed, "And Sir Harry Lauder himsel' sang accompanied by that pianna."

"Geez! Does the pianna sing as well?" Wullie was amazed.

"Don't be daft," Fingers said, continuing with the tout. He pointed to two silver objects in a plush case inside a display cabinet.

"Know whit they two things are, Wullie?" he asked. Wullie studied the objects but finally shook his head.

"Hivnae a clue," he said.

"That's a knife and fork," Wullie, Fingers said.

"Oh", was all that Wullie could reply. "You didn't need a knife and fork when you carried a fish supper wrapped up in a Daily Record."

"It's great even tae have yer ain lavvy!" Wullie said, "Ah couldnae help but notice it when we were in yer ... er ... distillery. And a real roll o' pink paper oan a brass holder oan the wa'! THAT, Fingers, is REAL luxury!" Wullie sighed. "We've jist got a nail in the wa' wi' square cut-oots o' the 'Record' or 'Times' stuck on it. Mind ye, it's got its advantages. Ye can get a wee read when ye're daein' yer thing. The only thing is, the printin' comes aff."

"Aye, well, Ah canny complain," Fingers said.

"Aye, ye've done well for yersel' Fingers," Wullie said with admiration. "If yer auld mother could only see ye noo, eh?"

Fingers nodded. "Aye, right enough", he said, "She never thought Ah'd live up a wally close. The only wally she was acquainted wi' wis her dugs oan the mantleshelf and her teeth. Still, she died a happy death."

"Ah thought she fell doon the stairs?" Wullie said, screwing up his eyes.

"She did," Fingers said, "but was as drunk as a monkey at the time."

Wullie nodded. He understood.

"Drink's a curse, Fingers!" Wullie said.

Fingers nodded.

"Aye, y're right, Wullie," he said, "here, try this." Fingers handed Wullie a glassful, "it's ma Piece De Resistance," he said proudly.

Wullie knocked back the drink and ran the back of his hand across his mouth.

"Aw, that was lovely, Fingers!" he said, "Whit was it?"

"Champagne, Wullie, ma ain recipe" Fingers said with pride in his voice.

"It is wonderful, Fingers!" Wullie repeated. "How did ye get that fizz intae it?"

"It's a matter o' gettin' the right amount o' gas intae it, Wullie," Fingers said.

"How dae ye dae that?" Wullie asked.

"Better no' askin', Wullie," Fingers said.

"Well, it's been an education," Wullie said, "An' Ah would be grateful if you would supply me wi' a few boattles for tae bring in the New Year wi', Fingers."

Fingers put an arm around Wullie's shoulder. "Ye know ma motto, Wullie," he said, "If ye're feelin' sad an' lonely, ye must have B.O. or, alternatively, ye'll feel a loat humbler when Ah fill yer tumbler!"

"Ye're a great man, Fingers," Wullie said, "and Ah would really be much obliged if ye could bring up some booze the night."

"Ah'll get the auld pipes workin' right away," Fingers promised, "an' Ah'll get the stuff roon' tae ye the night in plenty o' time for the bells ra morra night, so don't worry. Mind ye, it'll no' be Johnny Walker Red Label ye'll be gettin'. Mair like Johnny Crawler Purple Label."

"Whit dae ye call it that for?" Wullie asked, puckering his brow.

"Cos efter wan swig, that's the colour ye go," Fingers said.

"Fair enough!" Wullie said. "Ye never let us doon!"

"Ye know ma other motto, Wullie," Fingers said, hand on heart. "Naebody lingers when they come tae Fingers."

"Thanks Fingers," Wullie said making for the door, "See ye the night … and make sure ye empty the bath first … and don't bring any champagne."

Wullie almost skipped down Finger's stairs. Nothing could go wrong now and he would bring in the New Year as he was accustomed to doing.

He could already hear the gurgling and tappity-tapping of Fingers' wonderful contraption even before he reached the bottom of the stairs.

Naebody lingers when they come tae Fingers! Wullie whistled a happy tune as he walked out of the close and turned right towards Well Street.

Plooky Boyle was in the house when Wullie, whistling happily, arrived home. Plooky was wringing his hand – obviously nervous and agitated.

"Thank heavens youse were in!" he said to Rita and Rasputin. "There's been a terrible mistake. Ah've just discovered the hall wull no' be available on the 22nd efter a'!"

"Don't tell me it's for Auld Maggie Broon's maw's weddin' anniversary," Rita said facetiously.

"Don't be daft!" Plooky said, "that was last month. Naw … er … it's the roof. The workmen wull be in."

"Whit's up wi' the roof?" Rita asked worriedly.

"We're gettin' wan," Plooky said.

"Ah thought it was a bit draughty when we were there!" Rasputin said. "Ah just though it was 'Open Plan'."

"It couldnae be mair open," Plooky said.

"Was it a bomb?" Rita said.

"Naw, but somebody made a bomb, right enough," Plooky said, "They pinched the lead and wan night, during' a Barmitzvah, the wee boy was readin' oot how the Wa's o' Jericho came tumblin' doon when the rain came on and the roof blew aff."

"Good joab naebody was playin' a trumpet," Wullie said, "or ye might've loast yer wa's as well."

"That's terrible!" Annie said, putting the key in the door. "C'mon everybody, intae the hoose and we'll have a wee cuppa tea." Everybody piled in and Annie put the kettle on immediately.

Rita squeezed Rasputin's hand.

"Oh, whit are we gonny dae?" she wailed.

"Ah tell ye whit," Plooky said, "if ye can bring yer weddin' forward a wee bit, Ah'll help ye. Ye've got tae look efter oor fightin' men, efter a'. Ah could ask some o' the brides for tae postpone their weddins for tae help oot a sojer."

"Oh, that would be lovely!" Rita twittered.

"Mind ye there's no' many o' them could really postpone things for long!" Plooky said.

"When could ye gie them the hall, then?" Annie asked, knitting her brow.

"The morra!" Plooky said, "if youse don't mind sittin' doon wi' umbrellas … in case it rains."

"Oh, the morra's cuttin' it a bit neat!" Rita cried, "Oh mammy, whit will

Ah dae?" Annie put a comforting arm round Rita's shoulders.

"It's wartime, hen?" Annie said, "Time is precious and if this wee man says ye can have the hall the morra, go for it."

"Ah must dae ma bit for oor brave sojers," Plooky said. "Ah'd never forgive masel' if this young man here was suddenly called away and came back wi' his heid blawed aff."

"There's no much hope o' that," Wullie said, "cleanin' lavvies in Aldershot!"

"You hivnae seen some of the lavvies," Rasputin said.

Annie poured the tea and took command of the situation.

"Did ye hiv a cancellation or somethin'? she asked, peering over the lip of her cup.

Plooky nodded, "Aye," he said. "It was booked for Wee Minnie O'Flaherty's First Communion party but her da' cancelled it at the last minute."

"The wee sowel!" Annie commiserated. "Whit did he dae that for?"

"It was a' because Rangers cuffed Celtic twelve wan last week," Plooky said.

"Did he chinge his mind?" Annie asked,

"He changed his religion," Plooky said.

"Oh, well," Wullie said, "It must've been meant for tae be. Oor Rita gettin' married ... thanks tae Rangers ... noo, there's a turn up for the book, eh? And Annie never oot o' St Alphonsus's!"

"Aye, well God works in mysterious ways!" Annie said. Then, clapping her hands together, "Right", she said, "You two get away doon tae St Alphonsus's and see the priest. Noo, they're very good doon there and appreciate these situations."

"Oh, Ah'm that excited!" Rita said, clapping her hands and skipping on the spot. "Bu .. but .. oh, whit aboot transport?" she cried.

"Don't you worry aboot that, hen?" Curdy McVey said, "Ah wull pick youse up and get ye tae the chapel in plenty o' time for ten o'cloack mass ... that's the usual mass for weddins, int it?"

"Aye, that's right!" Annie said.

"It's awfu good o' ye Curdy," Rita said, pecking his cheek.

"Are ye sure it'll be a'right?"

"Nae bother!" Curdy said, "Ah've just wan wee joab in the moarnin' an' it entails me goin' tae St Alphonsus' anyway. Ah'll pick youse up here at quarter tae ten, right?"

"Lovely!" Rita cooed.

Annie took her coat from the door peg.

"Ah'll just go up and see how Mrs Cominsky's gettin' oan wi' yer weddin' dress, hen," Annie said.

"An' don't youse worry aboot the baun' or the cake," Plooky said, "Ah'll see tae that. Scruffy Duffy has always got a few spare cakes for emergencies."

"Jist as long as oor guests don't collapse haudin' their bellies!" Rasputin said.

"Wi' food poisonin', ye mean?" Wullie said, raising his brows.

"Woodworm", Rasputin said.

"Whit aboot oor guests?" Rasputin went on.

"It's no' gien' them much time!"

"If WE can make it, THEY can make it!" Rita said tugging his sleeve, C'mon!"

Rita ran down the stairs, happy and excited.

Annie had entered the Paddy close and gone round into the back court and up the stone steps, past the communal sink and water tap at the top of the stairs and on into the linoleumed long lobby. She stopped at Mrs Cominsky's door and prayed a silent prayer that the Well Street seamstress would be in.

The door opened immediately. Mrs Cominsky's ample proportions took up most of the aperture.

"Ah, Annie, you is a surprise!" she exclaimed.

"Aw, Mrs Cominsky," Annie blurted, "it's aboot ma Rita's weddin' dress …"

"Come in … come in," Mrs Cominsky said, opening the door wider. Annie entered and noted the treadle Singer's sewing machine already opened up in the centre of the floor.

"Ah have just been workin' hard oan it, Annie," the old lady said, "Oh Rita wull be a lovely bride!"

"The thing is," Annie said anxiously, "we need it right away…"

"For when?" Mrs Cominsky asked, narrowing her eyes.

"For the noo!"

Mrs Cominsky sat down at the machine.

"It's just as well that it's nearly finished, then, int it?"

Annie clapped her hands together.

"Aw, that's marvellous Mrs Cominsky!" Annie exclaimed.

"It just needs a press," Mrs Cominsky said, holding up the dress for Annie's approval, "Ah've tried tae get as many o' the swastikas oot as Ah could," she added, "there's only the odd wan here an' there ... especially under the oaxters."

"Aw, ye're a gem, so ye ur, Mrs Cominsky!" Annie gasped at seeing the silk wedding dress that was once a German parachute.

Rasputin and Rita had hurried along Stevenston Street until they arrived at St Alphonsus' Chapel House.

Father O'Malley, a big, jolly man, ushered them into the heavily carpeted lounge and indicated two chairs.

"Well, now," Father O'Malley said, after they were seated comfortably, "And what can I do for you at all, at all?"

"We MUST get married the morra!" Rita blurted out.

The priest's eyebrows shot up.

"Well, now, that's a very poignant statement!" he said. "I thought you were just puttin' on a bit of weight."

Rasputin laughed loudly and slapped his thigh.

"Aw ... Ah see whit ye mean," he said. "Naw, naw, the only club Rita's in is the Ruby Street Depot's social club."

"Thank heavens for that!" Father O'Malley exclaimed.

"Ah mean, we've only jist started kissin'," Rasputin went on.

"Rita's that shy, so she is. In fact we'd been goin the gether for eight months before she even affectionately bit ma ear."

"Had she no love in her heart?" Father O'Malley asked.

"Naw, she had nae teeth in her mooth," Rasputin said.

Father O'Malley stood up and, with his hands cupped round his back, walked slowly around the room, his eyes staring at the floor.

"What about the banns?" he said.

"Plooky Boyle's attending tae that," Rita said.

"Attending to the banns?" Father O'Malley said, raising his brows.

"Aye, an' the cake as well," Rita said.

"I'm talking about the reading of the banns from the pulpit," the priest said.

"Ah saw Father Hourigan here and he said it would be a' right," Rita said, concern creeping into her voice.

"Father Hourigan is on a retreat," Father O'Malley said.

"She didnae attack him!" Rasputin cried. "He didnae have tae retreat."

"A religious retreat," Father O'Malley said. "For a week o' prayin'."

"He obviously wisnae supportin' Celtic," Rasputin said.

"Well," the priest said, "if Father Hourigan okayed it, that's fair enough. Just one problem tomorrow. Ould Mrs McGinty will be gettin' carried into the chapel!"

"Wull she be drunk?" Rita asked.

"No, no," the priest said, "she's dead."

"An, she still goes tae mass?" Rasputin asked, puzzled.

"We keep her in overnight on a trestle before the holy altar before her funeral the next day. It's how we do things!"

"We'll just keep oot her road," Rasputin said.

"Very well," the priest said, "just as long as you don't mind the coffin bein' here."

"It's no' like she's gonny get up and dae a Highland Fling up an' doon the aisle, is it?" Rasputin said.

"Right, that's that settled," the priest said. "Now, would ye be wantin' Mrs O'Toole to play the organ for you?"

"Oh, that would be lovely!" Rita said "Here Comes the Bride" comin' in and "The Weddin' March" Da-da-dadadadada goin' oot," she hummed.

"Just pray that it doesn't rain," Father O'Malley said. "Otherwise the ould sowel's fingers stiffen up an all you're apt to get is Chopsticks."

Rita and Rasputin laughed, shook hands and bade the priest farewell. The happy couple immediately turned into Kent Street and on to London Road where they caught a number twenty-six "caur" going to Burnside. Ten minutes later they were getting off in Dalmarnock Road, near the Ruby Street depot. Rita breezed in to the canteen.

"Hello everybody!" she cried, "Jist in for tae put up a notice on the board."

Rita cadged a sheet of paper and a pencil from the desk clerk, wrote out her note and pinned it on to the notice board. Immediately she had left a crowd gathered to read the all important communication.

Rita invites all of youse to her wedding in St Alphonsus' Church, London Road (at the Barras) tomorrow at 10a.m. Thereafter to the Salamanca Street Hall, off Duke Street, near Parkhead Cross.

An excited buzz of conversation went round the crews and many wondered about the hurry of it all with the main comment, "She disnae look like she's put on any weight!" going its round.

Rita and Rasputin left them to their wonderment and comments and caught a car going west where they alighted at Well Street.

On entering the house there was a piercing scream as Annie dashed out and, grabbing Rasputin by the arm, pushed him towards a bedroom door.

"In there wi' you!" she cried, "You ur not supposed tae see yer bride's weddin' dress until ye're at the altar."

Rasputin grumbled but entered the bedroom, closing the door behind him.

"Oh mammy," Rita cried, "how is it? Ah mean, Mrs Cominsky is only used tae makin' patchwork quilts."

"It's lovely, hen!" Annie cried, "she has surpassed hersel'. If it wisnae for the swastikas ye'd never know it was a German parachute!"

"Aw, NAW!" Ah canny walk doon the aisle wi' a weddin' dress full o' swastikas, so Ah canny. Instead o' the priest raisin' his airm tae gie me a blessin' he'd be raisin' it and sayin' 'Heil Hitler.'

"Ye canny see the swastikas," Annie said, "There's jist a couple under yer oaxters. Unless ye raise yer haun if ye want tae go somewhere, naebody'll see them."

Mother and daughter entered the kitchen, where the wedding dress hung over the pulley.

Annie hurried over and lowered the spotless dress down and held it against herself.

"Look!" she cried.

Rita's hand came up to her mouth.

"Aw," she said, transfixed by the dress's beauty. "It's gorgeous!"

She walked slowly over to where Annie was pretending to be a mannequin. Taking the dress from her mother she held it to her cheek, purring at its soft silkiness.

"Tae think that this cloth was originally made to save somebody's life. And it still has done! It came doon frae the clouds and it's went right back up intae them again ... wi' me in it."

Annie stood back and watched Rita hold the dress close to herself and pirouette across the floor. Annie felt very proud and immediately thought of Big Sammy and wished with all her heart that he was there this day.

"Ye look beautiful, hen, like a film star!" Annie said, holding back a tear." Ah remember the day me and yer faither got married. Ah got a lovely wee two-piece suit at the Barras, wi' a Bristol Cheque and chinged intae it behind wan o' the stalls. Then it was just a metter o' goin' roon' the coarner and nippin' intae St Alphonsus.' Yer faither wore his best dungarees an' had borrowed a bowler hat. He looked that handsome! Then it was aff tae the Geggie, in Kirkpatrick Street and a boattle o' Tizer in the back row. In the darkness, he looked at me and telt me how lovely Ah looked in ma new, navy-blue two-piece suit and new teeth."

"Ye still look lovely, Mammy!" Rita said, kissing Annie's cheek.

"How did ye get oan wi' the priest?" Annie asked.

"Father Hourigan is away but the priest that was there says it would be a' right. Only problem is that an auld wumman called Mrs McGinty is gettin' brought in for tae lie at the altar."

"Aw, is auld Mrs McGinty deid?" Annie asked, surprised.

"Well, ah hope so, she's gonny be in a coaffin," Rita said.

"Poor auld sowel!" Annie said. She was a good age."

"She was ninety-six," Rita said, "Ah' Ah don't think that's a good age. AH'M twenty wan, noo THAT'S whit Ah call a good age tae be."

Annie laughed, "Aye, ye're right, hen," she said. "It's jist a figure o' speech. The poor auld sowel had a hard life, so she had. She steyed next door tae us when we first got married. Mrs Cominsky lived at the other side o' the landin' and, every Setturday night, we could SMELL the booze comin' frae next door. Her man used tae gie her laldy and then the next thing we heard was the furniture gettin' smashed an' her screamin' her heid aff. And it always ended up wi' the ambulance comin' an' her wee man gettin' certed aff tae the Royal Infirmary. Then, he was back hame oan Monday, his face a' stitched up in weird patterns. In fact Mrs Cominsky, when she started makin' patchwork quilts, swears she got her best patterns frae wee Mr McGinty's face." Annie sighed, "Ach well, that's her away noo, the auld sowel!"

"Whit happened tae her man?" Rita asked, her curiosity aroused.

"The wee nurse that took his stitches oot every week became the crochet queen o' Royston and they ran way the gether."

"Whit a sad endin'!" Rita said.

"Well, noo," Annie said, "The morra's yer big day, hen, eh?"

"Aye, ye jist take yer chances as they come alang these days," Rita laughed.

"Ah'll hurry doon tae Madame Wee Nellie's an' see if she can take me?" she said. "When Raspy gets up tell him Ah'll no' be long and that we'll have oor last wee fling at Barraland the night … oor last night bein' single."

Rita hurried out and Annie suddenly had the awful thought that some of the wedding guests might want to come back to the house after the reception. She immediately got her pinny on and started tidying up. She was glad that she'd already done the stairs.

At La Maison de petit Nellie, Coiffeuse to the Elite, Rita would get her hair done to look her best for Barrowland later in the evening and her big day to come.

Blonde and bouncy, Madame Wee Nellie, tongs in hand, leaned back in one of her operating chairs, feet up on the ledge and was smoking a Pasha.

Rita waved the smoke away from her face as she entered the shop. Nellie jumped up immediately and stubbed the cigarette out.

"Bon soir!" Nellie said.

"That pasha would put ye aff," Rita said,

"If Madamozell thinks that's putrid, wait till she tries moi's perfume. Noo, what does madamozell wish?"

"Ah'm aff tae Barraland the night," Rita said, "And Ah want ye tae tidy up ma hair."

Madame Wee Nellie studied Rita's crowning dome from every angle.

"Whit would you suggest, Madame Wee Nellie?" Rita went on.

"Merci," Nellie said, holding up her hand, "we haff no formalities here. Jist call me Nellie...forget the Madame Wee."

"Right!" Rita said, "Whit would you suggest?"

"A wig," Nellie said.

"Ah don't want a wig,"Rita said, "Ma fiancé would spot it right away. Ah want tae be natural."

"Oh, madamozell has got a fiancé?," Madam Wee Nellie cooed.

"Oh, aye, and we're gettin' married", Rita said. "But the night, we're goin' tae Barraland. You did ma neighbour's hair and made a good joab o' it."

"It must've been wan o' my good days," Wee Nellie said.

"Ye might remember her," Rita said, "Ina McLatchie?"

Madame Wee Nellie thought for a moment, tapping the side of her cheek with the tongs. "Ah, oui! " she cried "Eena McLatchie...a big wumman with ze baw face?"

"Aye, well Ah just like tae think it as a cheery face," Rita said.

"But of course I remember Big Eena McLatchie," Madame Wee Nellie enthused. "She was trying to trap ze man next door, eh? Voila! Wee Wullie, if I remember rightly. Did she get her man?"

"She's still tryin'," Rita said.

"Ah but she will ween!" Wee Nellie said. "I remember she wanted ze

Shirley Temple look but, her coupon being so beeg, I telt her it would be mair like ze Mormon Temple look."

"Aye, well she's a fighter," Rita said.

"Ah voila!" Nellie said, "I thought that when I saw ze condition her face was in. Is she heavyweight, oui?"

"Naw, Ah mean she's persistent," Rita said.

"Ah!" Nellie said. "And what about you, mon ami? Your fiancé, is he in ze armed forces, non?"

"Oh aye," Rita said, "He's advisor tae a very important man".

"What is your fiancé's name?" Madame Wee Nellie asked.

"Rasputin," Rita replied proudly.

"Oh!" Madame Wee Nellie said, bringing her hand up to her mouth. "And who is he advisor to...Stalin?"

"Naw, naw", Rita said quickly, "He is advisor tae General Montgomery. "Y'see, he's a genius." He invented a submarine that goes on top o' the watter."

"Is he a possible customer for me?" Wee Nellie asked.

"Whit dae ye mean?" Rita puckered her brows.

"Is he a heid case?" Nellie said.

"Indeed he is not," Rita said adamantly."He was always ahead for his years. But he had cruel parents. His faither used tae lay intae him every night wi' a cat o' nine tails."

"Tut-tut!" Madame Wee Nellie said shaking her head. "He widnae like that, eh?"

"Naw, and the cat wisnae pleased either," Rita said.

"What did the vee boy do?"

"He ran away frae hame tae earn his livin'."

"Lot's of vee boys do that," Madame Wee Nellie said.

"No' two year aulds, don't," Rita said.

"What about his mamon?" Nellie asked, sounding concerned.

"She was mair worried aboot the cat, because they had mice, y'see. The boy always came second in her affections. He craved for love and a neighbour wance saw him doon on a' fours tryin' tae catch a moose just so that he'd get noticed."

"And did he get noticed?" Nellie asked.

"Aye, the cat noticed and nearly tore his eyes oot," Rita said, "He wears glesses noo."

"I've never seen a cat wearin' specs," Nellie said.

"Naw, Raspy's wearin' glesses."

"But he sees YOU all right, eh?" Madame Wee Nellie said with a smile. "And he loves you. So, y'see he DID find love at last...even though he has been searchin' for it since he was two years old."

Rita nodded. "Aye, everythin' comes tae those who wait. Although it can sometimes be a long time."

"Whit age is he noo?" Madame Wee Nellie asked.

"Eighty six," Rita said.

Wee Nellie's brows shot up.

"That WAS a long wait. And, lookin' at you, it wisnae worth waitin' for."

"Whit dae ye mean by that?" Rita said, jumping up.

"Only kidden mon hen," Nellie said. "You could get a scone at any door."

"An' Ah'm only kiddin' aboot Raspy's age," Rita laughed, "He's jist a big, lovable boy."

"Aye, well, let's get back tae your hair,"Nellie said, "Whit aboot a perm?"

"Hey whit's happened tae yer French accent?" Rita cried.

"It's vanished under the sink with ze French Polish," Madame Wee Nellie laughed. "The nearest Ah've got tae France is visitin' ma pal, Maisie, in French Street, in Brigton," she went on.

"Ach it disnae matter anywey!" Rita said, " Ye don't have tae be French tae be a good hairdresser...or Italian tae be a good chippie. Ah knew a Brazilian who wisnae a nut."

"Right noo, let's have a look at this hair," Wee Nellie said. An hour later Rita was preening herself at the mirror.

"You're like ma Rasputin, Nellie," she said, "You're a genius. Rasputin loves Betty Grable and when he sees me the night, Ah'll put him in mind o' her."

"How is that?" Nellie asked.

"Ah look like Harry James," Rita laughed..."Only kiddin', mon poulet," she laughed. ""Ye'll get yer reward in heaven...as well as that tanner Ah left under that ash tray."

"Come back and Ah'll dae yer hair for nothin' for yer weddin'," Nellie called out as Rita stepped into the street.

"Thanks," Rita called back, "Ye're too late! But thanks again or should I say....MERCI?"

CHAPTER FOUR

Rita and Rasputin walked down Well Street and up towards Bain Square and the Gallowgate. Rita said nothing but she was a bit embarrassed by Raspy's attire. His German steel helmet glinted in the soft moonlight and the corner boys loitering around the Calton Social Club snapped to attention, raised their arms and, in chorus, chanted "Heil Hitler!" Rasputin ignored them. If Monty said it was okay, then it was okay by him.

There was a small queue at Barrowland and Raspy ignored the stares. The mellow music of the great Billy MacGregor Band wafted outside to the chill air of the Gallowgate where Rita and Rasputin queued, breathing warmth into their hands. Soon they were inside and Rita checked in her coat at the Ladies' cloakroom. Rasputin refused to hand in his tin hat in case it was "knocked". Some of the dancers didn't give him a second look, surmising the 'Big Yin' had thought he was going to a fancy dress night. Although some wags did click their heels and snap, 'Seig Heil'.

"C'mon, let's dance," Rita said steering him on to the well-polished floor. The band played "At Last", a popular Glen Miller number and the floor was packed with cheek-to-cheek dancers, all escaping into a dream world.

"Ah'm awfu' gled ye agreed tae come tae Barraland the night, Raspy," Rita whispered, "Ah thought ye might be too tired efter yer long journey frae Aldershot." Rasputin shook his head.

"Oh naw!" he said, "This is the best dancehall in Britain," he said, "An' yer hair's lovely, Rita...but dae ye have tae paint yer legs?"

Rita sniffled. "Ye jist canny get stoakin's, Raspy," Rita said, "A' the lassies paint their legs!"

"No purple, they don't," Raspy grunted. "Look at her ower here," he said, nodding towards one of the dreamers, " She's painted her legs tartan...Royal Stewart!"

"That's varicose veins Raspy," Rita said.

"Ach well, Ah'm here anywey..thanks tae General Montgomery," Rasputin sighed.

"Aw aye, it was awfu' good o' him gien' ye this leave," Rita twittered. "Was he nice, Raspy?"

Rasputin nodded.

"Oh aye," he said, "When Ah telt him ma plans for endin' the war, he nodded and leant back in his chair and started smokin'. THAT was very unusual for Monty, so it wis!"

"Whit's so unusual aboot that?" Rita asked.

"He wisnae puffin' oan anythin'," Rasputin said, his brows knitted.

"But he WAS nice tae, ye, eh? That's the main thing," Rita said.

"He couldnae've been nicer!" Rasputin said, "When Ah telt him that we were gettin' married and that you were findin' it hard tae get a weddin' dress, he telt me that you'd get wan in Rachman's department Store and that he knew for a fact that they were hivin' a sale of weddin' dresses. He suggested Ah surprise ye and go and get wan for ye. He said he'd gie me the coupons."

"AW, wisn't that nice!" Rita cried, "Where IS Rachman's, Raspy?"

"Nuremberg," Rasputin said, his brows knitting.

"But he gied ye leave anywey?" Rita sighed.

"Aye. And he even sent the sergeant major doon tae the station ta make sure Ah got a ticket...just a single, right enough, 'cos Ah think they're economisin'. And he telt me, that efter studyin' my plan, he wants me tae head the charge on the leadin' elephant," Rasputin sighed, pleased with himself.

"Ooh, that's wonderful, Raspy," Rita cooed, "tae have so much confidence in ye."

"An' ma plan," Rasputin added quickly.

"Och aye," Rita sighed, "Did ye hear ma da' was a prisoner o' the Japs?" she said softly.

"Aye, he'll no' like that," Rasputin said, shaking his head.

"Ah was hopin' that he might've escaped frae France and gied me away," Rita said trying not to fill up.

"How, whit have ye done?" Rasputin asked, puzzled.

"Ah meant that Ah was hopin' for him tae be there so that Ah could take his airm goin' doon the aisle."

"How? Ur ye plannin' tae be drunk?" Rasputin quizzed.

"It's the CUSTOM, Raspy," Rita said in frustration. "Ah'll bet your maw's faither gied her away."

"Aye, right enough," Rasputin said, "She stole her weddin' dress oot o' Fraser's windae and she asked her da' tae gie her away and he did and she got six months."

"It's no' the same thing, Raspy," Rita said, despair in her voice.

They didn't notice the American soldier approaching.

"HEY, it's YOU again," he drawled, "Betty Grable...remember me...that last time I was here? Mind if Ah have this dance, buddy?" he said, looking at Rasputin.

"Ah don't dance wi' men," Rasputin replied with a grimace.

"No, I meant with the lady."

"It's okay by me," Rasputin said, "but nae gum!"

Rita and the G.I. danced off to the sound of "In The Mood". "Ya remember me, baby?" he said.

Rita nodded.

"Oh aye!" she said, "Yer name's Hank, int it?"

"You got it, babe," Hank said, swinging her round in time to the music. "It's great to be back here in Glasgow, although I miss ma maw's home cookin'...blueberry pie...the Brooklyn Dodgers...you don't have anythin' like the Brooklyn Dodgers here, do ya?"

"Naw, jist jammy dodgers..and fare dodgers," Rita said.

"Yeah, there's nothin' Ah liked better than gettin' up in the mornin', eatin' ma pancakes smothered in maple syrup and steppin' out and breathin' in that cool, clean Texan air. Then Ah'd ride the range and blow the cobwebs away...clear the head. How does that appeal to ya, baby, eh?"

"No really! If AH had tae ride the range first thing in the mornin' a' Ah'd get is ma erse a' blacklead," Rita yawned.

Hank burst out laughing and they swept on around the floor.

Rasputin's eyes narrowed as he saw Rita and the G.I. laughing but his thoughts were interrupted by a girl's voice.

"Come on, Shorty," she said, "ye look lonely staunin' there. C'mon an' dance."

Before he could argue, Rasputin' was almost pushed on to the dance floor. The blonde girl barely came up to Rasputin' waist as they caught up with 'In The Mood'.

"That's a right funny uniform ye've got on," she said.

Rasputin' chest puffed out.

"This is a very special uniform gied to me by General Montgomery. It's a protection against the terrible contagious disease what Ah've got."

The girl drew away.

"Ter...Terrible disease?" she stammered.

"Aye, but don't worry aboot it, "Rasputin said reassuringly, " "Ye canny get smitted as long as Ah'm wearin' this gear."

"Whi..whi..whit's yer disease called.?", the frightened girl asked.

"Measles," Rasputin said.

"An' ye've got tae wear that uniform for tae contain it?" the girl asked with incredulity.

Rasputin nodded,

"Aye," he said, "it's German measles."

"Ah'm beginnin' tae get suspicious aboot you," the girl said, "that looks like a German uniform tae me."

"Clothes don't make the man," Rasputin said, "Ah'll let you know that Ah'm a good Scotsman frae the Calton...although born in Govan."

"Whit's yer name?" the girl asked quizically.

"Rasputin."

"You should be shot wi' a name like that," the girl said.

"You should be shot wi' a face like that," Rasputin answered. The girl took umbrage, stamped her foot and walked off the dance floor.

Hank saw the encounter from the middle of the floor.

"Is your friend a kraut?" he asked Rita.

Rita shook her head.

"Naw, he's a catholic," she said.

"No, Ah meant...that's a kraut's uniform. Does he think this is fancy dress night?"

"Naw,naw," Rita said, "THAT'S his weddin' suit."

"Who's his tailor....Herman Goering?" Hank said facetiously.

"His uniform was gied tae him through a general..."Rita said.

"Through a general clearance?" Hank sniped.

Rasputin's jealousy reached boiling point. Striding into the centre of the dance floor, he took Rita's arm.

"C'mon, Rita" he commanded, "we'd better get hame an' prepare for oor weddin!"

Rita nodded, "Aye, right enough," she said. They began to walk off but Rita stopped, turned and facing the G.I., said: "Yer name might be Hank, but ye don't pull any wool ower MA eyes. Ah DAE know that ye don't get the Brooklyn Dodgers in Texas.In fact your team in Texas is called efter wan o' oor teams....Rangers....We've got the Glasgow Rangers, you've got the Texas Rangers. So, maybe we DAE have somethin' in common efter a' Goodnight, Hank and a Happy New Year when it comes...and Ah hope ye'll be hame soon wi' yer maw and her blueberry pie.. Noo, that's a pie OOR Rangers boys would enjoy, Ah'm sure."

Hank laughed and waved and Rasputin and Rita stepped out into the chill night air of Gallowgate....and it chased the cobwebs away.

Rita hung on closely to Rasputin as they hurried along Gallowgate, turning right into Kent Street and on up and into London Road.

"Oh, Ah'm freezin'!" Rita complained. Passing St Alphonsus Church, Rita said, "Ah went in there the day an' lit a caunle!"

"That widnae keep ye waarm," Rasputin said.

"Naw, it wisnae tae keep me warm," Rita said, "It was for spiritual heat. Ah had tae see Father Hourigan aboot oor weddin'. But it was Fr. O'Malley ah saw!"

Rasputin smiled at his gaffe. They hurried on along London Road.

"C'mon in here," Rita said as they arrived at Peter Rossi's cafe.

They were glad to get inside out of the biting wind.

"A plate o' hoat peas," Rita ordered. "Same for me," Rasputin said.

The steaming plateful of peas on which they sprinkled a liberal amount of salt, pepper and vinegar arrived.

"Oh, that's lovely an' hoat," Rita said with delight at her first mouthful.

"So it is," Rasputin agreed.

They finished the delicacy with relish and ordered a cup of tea.

"Sorry, we've nae biscuits," the young waitress said.

They sipped the hot, sweet tea, Rita holding the cup in her cupped hands.

"It's a right clear sky the night," she said, "and a big moon. Dae ye think we'll get a visit the night, Raspy?"

"Well, it's jist the kind o' night the Luftwaffe like," he said knowingly.

"But it's almost Hogmanay," Rita complained.

"Ideal for them," Rasputin said, "They'll think that we're a' relaxed and pie-eyed...off oor guard, know whit Ah mean? We'll need tae be vigilant."

Rita took in every word Rasputin was saying. He's so knowledgeable, she thought.

She was so happy to have him with her. And she thought of her father, Big Sammy a million miles away from his family. She didn't know what suffering he might be going through. But she knew the suffering her mother was nursing. She could relate to it now that she had a love of her own. At least, in France, there was always a chance of escape. But that seemed impossible now. Still Big Sammy was expert at getting out of tight situations!

They clinked cups.

"Tae us, hen, tae us...and the end o' this damned war," Rasputin said.

"Aye, an' tae ma da'...that he comes through it," Rita added.

They finished their tea on a sombre note.

There was a whoop of delight from behind the counter. The young waitress jumped up, waving something in the air.

"Hey, look whit Ah found!" she hollered, coming round to Rita and Rasputin's table.

"Look, a packet o' Abernethy biscuits."

She danced as though she had found gold at the end of the rainbow.

"Here...wan each for the two lovebirds!"

Rita and Rasputin accepted the biscuits with gratitude.

"See," Rita said, "Maybe oor luck's chingin' right enough!"

Geraldo and his Orchestra were playing 'I'll be Seeing You' on the wireless.

"That song always makes me greet!" Annie said, dabbing her eyes with the corner of her 'peeny'.

"Never mind, Annie, everythin' wull turn oot a'right," Ina said, "Just you wait an' see!"

"It didnae for you," Annie said, scowling at Wullie, who averted his eyes and gave the Evening Times a shake, continuing to read.

Ina smiled.

"Ye KNOW Wullie's a confirmed bachelor," she said.

But Annie was angry at Wullie's treatment of Ina. She had thought that Wullie might settle down now that Ina's father had passed on. For a time it did look that way. She had seen them holding hands in the air-raid shelter the night Rita and Rasputin got engaged. The night that Big Mario Valente had saved the day by walking into the shelter with a basketful of steaming hot fish suppers for the engagement party guests after the pig Fingers McGeachie had acquired was carted off to Tobago Street police office by the ever alert Erchie McPherson.

But Wullie had reneged and everything was as it was before.

"You led that lassie on, so ye did," Annie snapped, unable to contain herself any longer. "Ye should be ashamed o' yersel'!"

Wullie continued to read his paper.

"Ah canny be bought for a couple o' soday scones," he said without looking up.

Ina had baked a plateful of soda scones for Wullie, knowing it was his favourite delicacy. And, for a time, it looked like that had swayed things Ina's way. But Wullie's taste of love vanished after the last bite.

"Ina made they scones tae please YOU, ya selfish get!" Annie snapped. "Jist look at the lovely lassie. Ye's lucky she even looks at YOU. Whit's wrang wi' her. A'right, she might be a wee bit overweight...but you've got a fat heid. YOU are fortunate, Wullie McSorley, that any young, attractive wumman, like Ina, even looks at ye. In fact you'd be lucky if any ugly young wumman looked at ye. And ye'd even be lucky if any AULD wumman looked at ye."

"He'd be lucky if any auld MAN even looked at him," Ina chuckled.

"Ah don't like her long, red hair!" Wullie snapped.

"Rita Hayworth's got long, red hair," Annie said.

"No' comin' doon her nose, she's no'!" Wullie rapped back.

"Away ya ignorant get!" Annie growled.

"Ma da' would've thrown you doon the stairs if he had heard you sayin' a thing like that," Ina cried.

"YOUR Da'?" Wullie scoffed, "YOUR da couldnae even walk up they stairs. He used tae stagger oot the Come Inn and bounce aff the wa's. He had tae get Wee Abe Goldberg and Wee Rueben Woolfson tae CAIRRY him up the stairs...the whole three flights, that stotious, he was. They two should've got a medal for their efforts in gettin' your da' hame safely!"

Annie's brows shot up.

"How should they get a medal?" she boomed, "Abie and Rueben were only daein' their Christian duty in helpin' an auld man up the stairs."

"They're only five years auld, Annie," Wullie said in a flat monotone.

"Ah don't believe it!" Annie said.

"Believe it if ye like," Wullie retorted, "but Wee Rueben's the only five year auld wean in the street wi' a hernia."

"Ma faither was a great star in Hollywood," Ina said quickly. "Everybody in Hollywood loved him..even Rin-Tin-Tin, the great dug actor. They two were inseparable efter they made that picture together... 'Rin-Tin-Tin meets Pluto'."

"Did yer faither play 'Pluto'?" Wullie asked sarcastically.

"Ma da' played the lead," Ina said without realising the implication of what she had said.

"Well, he's away noo and it's jist as well his ashes wurnae scattered in the windae boax as was intended," Wullie said. "Wan good gust o' wind and he'd hiv been flyin' aboot gettin' up everybody's nose jist like he did when he was living."

Wullie had collected Old Jake McLatchie's ashes from the undertaker with the view to scattering them in the window box, as was his wish. But, on his way home, Wullie had left the earthenware jar with the powdered Jake on top of the Come Inn counter. And it was knocked over and smashed by Dougal,the pub dog, sending the ashes down the sink and en route to Rothesay.

At Jimmy Smith, the barman's suggestion, Wullie had filled a pint glass with soot and pretended it was the late Mr McLatchie and duly sprinkled 'him' in the window box.

"Never mind HIM," Annie said, "it's HIM that gets up everybody's nose. He couldnae get a wumman if he tried!"

Wullie's eyebrows shot up.

"Is that so!" he snapped, "Let me tell youse that when Ah was in the army , in France, in 1915, Ah fell in love wi' this wee mademoiselle".

"Frae Armentieres?" Annie said sarcastically.

"She wis originally frae the Po Valley," Wullie said, "although she wisnae a chanty wrastler. We would've got married only for wan thing." Wullie sighed.

"An' whit was that?" Ina asked, folding her arms and staring Wullie straight in the eye.

"She couldnae staun' the sight o' me," Wullie said with a sad note.

"Ah!" Annie piped up, "Whit did Ah tell ye..could never get a wumman."

"Naw, naw," Wullie cried, " we soon sorted that oot. She needed new specs. She saw me as a blur."

"Lucky for her!" Ina commented.

Wullie ignored the remark.

"We only found oot aboot her poor eyesight when, wan day, Ah was hivin' a bath and clappin' ma hauns in time tae the music on the wireless, when she came in and threw me a fish."

"That SEALED yer love, eh?" Annie said facetiously.

"Very funny!" Wullie said. "She was angry when Ah didnae catch it in ma mooth.Anywey, she apologised and, efter a new pair o' specs, that was the end o' the romance."

"Hah! There ye are, then," Annie cried, "She got new specs and threw you over, eh?"

"Naw, AH got new specs," Wullie said, "And saw that she looked like Daphne Broon and that was it. Ah immediately asked tae be put up tae the front line."

"Just think, Wullie," Ina said, "you could've been a Frenchman by noo."

"Aye," Annie said, "instead o' bein' a Monsewer, he's just an ordinary sewer. Anywey," she said, rising and taking her coat from the hook on the door, "Ah'm away doon tae Mary Welsh's tae see if she got any tea in... Ah'll no' be long...and nae fightin' between you two..right?" Annie left and here was a long pause.

"Dae ye no' see ANYTHIN' attractive aboot me, Wullie?" Ina said at last.

"Yer left leg's no' bad," Wullie replied

"Annie thought it was time that you should get spliced and Ah volunteered."

"Volunteered for whit?" Wullie asked, puzzled.

"Ah thought she said 'SLICED', Ina said without smiling.

"Humph!" Wullie grunted.

"But wan o' you is enough, Wullie." Ina went on, "Ah widnae mairry you if ye went doon on yer bended knee!"

"ME? GO DOON ON MA BENDED KNEE?" Wullie cried, That is wan thing ye'll never see...ME goin' doon on ma bended knee."

"Ah know that, Wullie," Ina said, " Ye'd be frightened ye couldnae get up again."

"Ur you suggestin' Ah'm gettin' auld?" Wullie exploded.

"Gettin' auld?" Ina cried, "Wullie...look in the mirror. Have a gander at yer face. Ye've got mair lines than Eddie Trainer, the bookie."

"That is character,"Wullie retorted, "THAT is a 'lived-in' face, so it is!"

"Aye, well ye've got squatters, Wullie," Ina answered.

"Ah could get any wumman Ah want up this street," Wullie said haughtily.

"Ye'll never get them up the close, that's for sure," Ina replied. "Ye're just a blether, Wullie. Ah'm no' gonny hing aboot waitin' for ye. There's plenty o' other fish in the sea...and Ah'm no' talkin' aboot the kind that that Medamoiselle tossed at ye in the bath."

Wullie was about to reply when the droning voice of Lord Haw-Haw interrupted the music on the wireless.

"Germany Calling..Germany Calling," the dull monotone repeated, "Good evening Glasgow. I see The Thief of Baghdad is on at the Greens

Playhouse, in Renfield Street,this weekend.Of course you will be afraid to go in case our glorious Luftwaffe should pay you a visit."

The voice droned on as Ina rose and headed for the door.

Turning, she said..."Tell Annie Ah couldnae wait. Ah was gettin' bored.." Nodding towards the radio, she added, "Ye remind me o' him, Wullie. Ye talk a lot o' rubbish. Cheerio!"

Ina slammed the door leaving Wullie with his mouth open. Rising, he stormed over to the wireless and angrily switched it off.

"Ach, shut up you," he snarled.

Rita had arrived home from Barrowland tired but happy. She tossed and turned all night, too excited to sleep. She remembered the dream she once had about her wedding where her dress resembled a patchwork quilt and, as she walked down the aisle, her favourite singer, Bing Crosby, stood up on the pulpit and sang "I'm dreaming of a White Wedding." Now it was all coming true! Only Mrs Cominsky had done a job that would have done the Paris Fashion houses proud.

She hoped it wouldn't rain and thought that she should have warned her clippie colleagues to arm themselves with umbrellas at Plooky's Place.

Rita closed her eyes and sleep finally enveloped her. Annie was already up when Rita opened her eyes.

"Right, hen," Annie said. "Nae breakfast for you this moarnin' if ye're goin' tae Holy Communion. Up ye get!"

Rita rose and washed herself at the sink. Annie had boiled up a kettle and run water from the cold tap into the basin, testing it with her elbow, making sure her daughter would not be scalded.

"Ah used tae dae this for you when ye were a baby," she laughed. An hour later and Rita stood before the bedroom mirror.

"Ye're jist a picture, hen," Annie said, dabbing her eyes.

"An' ye're lookin' lovely yersel', mammy!" Rita said, admiring Annie's two-piece navy blue suit.

Wullie entered wearing his dark brown gaberdine suit which he retrieved from the Kent Street pawn shop yesterday evening.

"How dae AH look?" he said, posing.

"Aw, ye're right handsome, Uncle Wullie," Rita said, pecking his cheek. "Like Gary Cooper."

"Mair like Gladys Cooper," Annie sniped, "Ye should've got yer hair cut," she scolded.

"Ah hudnay time tae waash ma heid!" Wullie complained.

The conversation was stopped by the abrupt blasting of a motor's horn. Wullie hurried over to the window and peered out.

"It's Curdy!" he said, "C'mon," He crooked his arm and offered it to Rita and his other, for Annie. Wullie whistled jauntily as he escorted the two women in his life down the stairs.

"Hey, whit aboot me?" They stopped and looked up as Ina McLatchie hurried down the stairs.

"Aw Ina, ye look lovely!" Annie said.

Ina beamed.

"Dae ye think so?" she twirled. "As soon as Ah saw this lilac froack Ah knew it was just meant for me. Ma da' always said lilac was ma colour."

"It goes wi' yer eyes, right enough!" Wullie said, followed by an "Ouch"! as Annie kicked his ankle.

"Thanks for askin' me to be yer Best Maid, Rita," Ina said.

"Ah know it was a bit short notice, Ina," Rita said.

"Ye still gied me time for to get ma dress," Ina said.

"Did it exhaust yer clothin' coupons?" Rita asked with some concern.

"Not wan coupon did it cost me," Ina said with a smile of satisfaction.

"Oh, that was good!" Annie said, "Where did ye get it, the C&A?"

Ina shook her head. "Naw," she said, "The P.M."

"P.M.?" Annie screwed up her nose, puzzled.

"Paddy's Market," Ina cried. "The man on the stall said it wance belanged tae a famous Hollywood female star. AH think he was hintin' it was Betty Grable."

Probably Rin-Tin-Tin," Wullie said.

"Oh, don't mention Rin Tin Tin," Ina said, her hankie coming up to her eye.

"Oh aye, Ah forgot," Wullie sighed, "That's the dug that gave yer auld man rhumatics in his left leg."

"Naw, he said it wance belanged tae a famous Hollywood ACTRESS."

"Well, it widnae be an ACTOR, would it?" Wullie said, adding, "Oh, Ah don't know ..."

The quartet carried on down the stairs with Ina commenting how clean and smelling of disinfectant they were. Annie's chest expanded three inches.

They stepped out into the street on a bright, sunny morning. A crowd of "weans" had gathered for the scramble. The word had gone out. Rita stopped in her tracks, her jaw fell open and misery swept over her.

Curdy McVey sat at the wheel of the highly polished hearse, his tile hat glinting in the sunshine. He beamed a wide smile when the wedding party came into the street. Behind him lay the brown, oak coffin containing the mortal remains of Mrs Clementina McGinty.

Rita's shaking finger pointed at the coffin.

"Whi ... whi ... whit's that?" she stammered.

"Ah telt ye Ah had a wee job on this mornin'. Ah had tae go tae the Royal and pick up Auld Mrs McGinty for her lyin' in the aisle o' St Alphonsus' before her final planting," Curdy said.

"Ah am not turnin' up for ma weddin' in a hearse," Rita sobbed.

"Especially wan wi' a deid boady in it."

"Please yersel'," Curdy said. "If ye want tae wait, Ah'll nip alang tae the chapel and get Mrs McGinty on tae her trestle."

"Aye, ye dae that, Curdy, you dae that!" Rita said.

Curdy started the engine, much to the dismay of the "Scramble gang." Rita, Wullie, Annie and Ina, retreated up the stairs again and waited.

Curdy McVey pulled up outside St Alphonsus' chapel, in London Road. In the front pew, Rasputin stood waiting, nervously twisting his medal and too frightened to look back. Curdy caught the attention of the passkeepers, who came to his assistance in taking Mrs McGinty from the hearse and propping her up on their shoulders. Father O'Malley had come out from the Sacristy and stood at the altar, Good Book in hand.

In the choir loft, Old Mrs O'Toole's fingers were supple thanks to the good weather. Immediately she saw Father O'Malley take his place at the front of the altar, she struck up "Here Comes the Bride". The music boomed all over the church and Rasputin, unable to contain himself and eager to see his lovely bride, turned his head and looked up the aisle ... as Curdy McVey and three of the passkeepers solemnly carried the coffin of Mrs McGinty. The music reached a crescendo and Rasputin fainted on the spot. Father O'Malley immediately sent one of the altar boys up to the choir loft to shut Mrs O'Toole up.

Curdy wasted no time in depositing Mrs McGinty atop of the funeral trestles and sped back the few hundred yards to Well Street.

Rita was relieved to see that the coffin had been disposed of and stepped daintily into the cab of the hearse, followed by Annie, Wullie and Ina who had to squeeze in as best they could.

Old Mrs O'Toole, hands poised above the key board watched and waited. At last the signal came as Wullie, with Rita on his arm, walked proudly down the aisle. Mrs O'Toole's fingers crashed down on the keyboard and the pipes of the huge organ blasted into life ... "Abide With Me" echoed round the church with Rita now dabbing her eyes.

The tears welled up when she arrived at the front of the altar to see Father O'Malley down on his knees and wafting smelling salts under the prostrate body of Rasputin.

"Aw, thank heavens ye're no' deid!" Rasputin murmered when he, at last, opened his eyes.

The wedding went ahead with Ina tearfully carrying through her duties. Now and again she would look pleadingly over at Wullie, who immediately turned away and avoided her loving gaze.

The ceremony over, Rasputin crooked his arm and he and his new bride walked up the aisle to the strains of "The Lord Is My Shepherd" being played by the agile fingers of Mrs O'Toole.

The Well Street children had followed the hearse, robbed of their scramble and were ready to give Wullie, who, had forgotten the all-important ritual, a hostile reception when he appeared at the door of the church. Wullie took in the situation immediately and called over the obvious leader of the pack. Digging into his pocket, he produced a fistful of pennies and ha' pennies ... with a few silver "Thrupennies" thrown in.

He remembered how he, himself, used to look forward to local weddings and the scrambles. And, usually about nine months later, although sometimes sooner, the bride of the time would have a wee addition to her family.

Wullie would hang around the close-mouth waiting for the baby to come down the stairs in its Godmother's arms, on the way to its Christening. His eager wee hand stretched out to grab the piece of buttered bread ... with a half-crown inside as was the custom. Wullie called over the boy who looked liked the leader of this pack. "Look, son," he said, "it's too dangerous for me tae throw yer scramble here, in London Road. Dae ye want just tae take these coppers and divide them oot or wull we go roon' the coarner tae Kent Street and Ah'll toss them in the air."

"Kent Street", the boy said, wiping his nose with his sleeve.

"'He's no' fool, this boy,' Wullie thought to himself. 'He knows that he'll be the winner in any scramble. God help anybody who would dare get in his way during the scrum!"

"Right!" Wullie said, "C'mon. Ah'll no' be a minute," he called to Curdy and Rita who, with Annie, Ina and Rasputin were crushing into the cab.

The scramble went as Wullie expected with the ragamuffin's elbows digging in deeply. Wullie wasted no time and was back round the corner and squeezing as best he could into the cab.

Ina was still waiting and Wullie handed her a crisp, white hankie Annie had ironed for him the previous night.

"Shut yer Geggie, wull ye!" he cried. "Wan o' these days it'll be you goin' doon that aisle. A-La oor Rita or Mrs McGinty. So, let's enjoy the day."

Annie wept through most of the service! Tears streamed down her cheeks when she saw her beautiful Rita standing at the altar, radiant in her German parachute and Rasputin holding her hand with one hand and polishing his medal with the other.

In a wave of happy and sad nostalgia, she found herself going back through the years and Rita was a little girl again. Annie remembered their poverty, of how they sub-leased a single-end in Langlands Road, in Govan, above Galls, the draper's. How, with Rita's first day at school looming, she had nothing decent to give the wee girl to wear. She felt ashamed climbing the stairs, Rita clutching tightly to her hand, at the Parish office where she would bare her soul and had all dignity stripped from her. But it was a little girl, in her innocence, who walked proudly into St Anthony's School that first morning wearing a neat navy-blue gym slip, dark woollen socks, with a red band and a pair of shiny, sturdy shoes on her feet. To wee Rita, no trousseau could have been more beautiful.

Big Sammy had been working in Fairfields' Shipyard then but had to leave due to a disputed industrial accident when he caught a red-hot rivet in his mouth.

Sammy arrived home that day and found it difficult to tell Annie what had happened. His teeth had melted. Annie immediately found a part-time job in a fishmonger's in Govan Road.

Sammy and Annie would leave together early in the morning and, while Annie went to the Fishmonger's shop, Sammy went job hunting. Arriving home in the afternoon, he would wonder if Annie was home before him and have some food, usually fish, on the table.

Jobs were hard to find and Sammy went the way of many others by singing round the backcourts of Govan. Housewives knew when it was "Sammy's Day" for their backcourts and neighbourhood dogs and cats deserted in droves. A good day would earn him two shillings and at least three jeely pieces. Although once a kind housewife, from her three-storey house, threw over a half-pound of mince – cooked.

Annie continued to pray for her own wee home and it was once, when she went over to St Alphonsus' Church, in London Road, for a novena, she heard of a single-end going at 27 Well Street, *near* the 'Barras'. One of the church's passkeepers, Sandy McBride, knew the factor and it was with pride that Annie watched Sammy sign the missive of let.

The house, which had been lying empty for a while, was very popular. Four thousand mice had moved in but, fortunately, one of the Govan cats had followed Annie over to the Calton. It had a field day and the mouse population decreased at an amazing rate.

Later a larger house became vacant up the close, when Old Mrs McWhachle was found dead in her chair with a Lysol bottle at her feet. She had apparently mistaken the lysol for her bottle of ipecacuanha wine.

Annie and family moved into the three room and kitchen and, although the rent was a bit higher, Annie merely rolled up her sleeves and took in more washing.

It was then that her brother, Wullie, who had fought in World War One, with the Highland Light Infantry, asked if he could come and live with them Sammy had no objection as not only was he related to Wullie through Annie, they were also related through drink. Wullie's contribution to the family budget would be of enormous help. His thigh had been chipped by a bullet and he was on a war pension. Rita had taken to her 'Uncle Wullie' right away and to him, she was the apple of his eye.

Sammy gave up singing and, after trying his hand at busking outside the King's Cinema, in James' Street, he gave that up, too, when somebody stole his bunnet … with his takings.

Rita grew up and had joined the Glasgow Corporation Transport Department as a conductress on 'the Caurs' and had met Rasputin Plunkett when he boarded her tram in London Road, with a roll of linoleum he had just purchased at the 'Barras'. It was love at first sight especially when Rasputin turned out to be a great dancer during their visits to Barraland.

Wullie had been a strong shoulder and, although they bickered a lot, Annie was very fond of her brother. Her only wish was that he could find himself a good woman to look after him. Big Ina McLatchie, from next door, had tried hard to get him interested but to no avail. Wullie was set in his ways. Time, Annie thought, for another novena.

Father O'Malley concluded the service and Rita was now Mrs Plunkett.

Annie sent a scowl up to the choir loft as they left the church but Mrs O'Toole played on, unaware.

Curdy turned the hearse around and headed down Kent Street, into Gallowgate where he turned right and speeded on up towards Parkhead Cross. Then left into Duke Street, past the Granada Cinema and down towards the mighty Parkhead Forge, turning right into Salamanca Street. Rita prayed that the rain would stay off and, as Curdy screeched to a stop outside the hall, Annie let out a cry. Her hand came up to her mouth.

"Aw naw!" she cried, "Know whit we forgot?" She didn't wait for an answer. "We've got nuthin' tae gie them tae eat!" she wailed.

But, on entering the hall, to be met by a smiling Plooky Boyle, Annie's jaw dropped as she saw three rows of long tables set out with brightly coloured crepe paper covering them and with cups, saucers and plates laid neatly out. Rita noted, too, that the roof was covered by a heavy tarpaulin.

Plooky, being the gallant wee man that he was, took Rita's hand and planted a long on kiss on it.

"Welcome, hen and wishin' you every happiness. Ah borrowed the tarpaulin frae Auld Allison, the demolishers, just in case we should get a spit o' rain."

"Bu ... bu ... but the tables?" Annie blurted out.

"Compliments o' the wee lassie's faither who had booked the hall for her First Communion do. He had sent the stuff up in advance. Ah believe he was related tae Auld McPhee, who used tae have a grocer's shop doon near Well Street but got demolished in the blitz."

Annie and Rita's eyes met and they burst out laughing.

"That's justice for ye, right enough!" Annie laughed. "It was Auld McPhee's bombin' that did us oot o' Rita's grub for her engagement. Ah'd been savin' up ma food coupons wi' him and we loast the lot!"

"Aye, well, that's justice, right enough!" Plooky said.

Happy guests arrived, mostly from the Ruby Street tram depot, and Rita and Rasputin welcomed them. Many commented on Rasputin's medal ... the Iron Cross, First Class, which he had polished up to gleaming perfection. Everybody gasped at Rita's beautiful wedding dress and were amazed that it had been made from a parachute. After a meal of corned mutton and boiled potatoes, a toast was given by Wullie from some alcoholic beverages acquired by Plooky Boyle and his associates from dubious sources.

"We are here for to wish ma wee niece, Rita and her new husband, Rasputin, a' ra best for ra future," he said, staggering slightly, having sampled Plooky's booze earlier.

"The war wull soon be ower noo that Rasputin has taken up the colours. For he is undoubtedly a genius," he went on.

Rasputin blushed and Rita proudly squeezed his arm.

Speeches over, the band turned up and the dancing began. Barney's Bachles were in great demand and once played in the City Chambers for the Lord Provost during a charity drive. They were also well established with the local Orange Lodge and the Hibernian Society with a repertoire to suit both organisations – from 'The Sash My Father Wore' to 'Faith of Our Fathers'. Annie found herself dancing 'The Pride of Erin' with Plooky, who was light on his feet and complimented by Annie, who loved dancing and remembered her own days at the Dennistoun Palais and 'Barraland.'

"Ye're a real wee Fred Astaire, Plooky!" she commented.

"Ah learnt dancin' at the Albert where Ah used for tae frequent oaften," Plooky said proudly. "A' the best dancers came frae the Albert!" he added.

"Naw, naw," Annie said, shaking her head. "Barraland was THE place for tae learn everythin' frae a quck-step tae a tango."

They agreed to differ.

"Ye know, Plooky", Annie said, knitting her brows, "somethin's been worrying me!"

"Oh? Plooky said, "Whit's that, then?"

"The wee lassie who should've been here the day … she must be terribly disappointed!"

Plooky shook his head.

"Naw, naw!" he said, "Her faither had a remorse o' conscience and when Ah telt him that Ah'd agreed for tae gie you the hall for yer daughter's weddin' tae a servin sojer, he telt me for tae leave things be. He got a len' o' the Sacred Heart Hall, in Muslin Street, that jist happened tae be free the day."

Annie sighed with relief. She remembered her own First Communion and how she enjoyed the party afterwards with sticky buns and lemonade.

"Ah'm gled everythin' turned oot well!" she said.

Wullie danced a waltz with Rita, managing to keep from stepping on her toes and avoiding Ina McLatchie.

"Ye're lookin' lovely, hen!" he said with sincerity. "Where are youse goin' frae here?"

"We're goin' straight hame," Rita said, "Ina is takin' ower ma room the night and gien' Raspy and me her hoose. Int that nice o' her?"

Wullie was dubious.

"Ah'd better padlock ma door the night in that case," he said with a wry smile.

Barney's Bachles played a Canadian Barn Dance with the whoops and cries almost blowing the tarpaulin off the roof.

Rita and Rasputin had found themselves a secluded corner where they sat, holding hands and in deep conversation.

"Well, that's it, hen!" Rasputin said, "yous are now Mrs Plunkett … ma ain wee wife!"

"Aye, a bit o' a rush, but everythin's turned oot well," Rita sighed, "but Ah'm just a wee bit worried, Raspy?" she said drawing her eyebrows together.

"Whit are ye worried aboot, Rita?" Raspy squeezed her hand.

"Where are we gonny live?" Rita said, "Ah've got oor name doon in the Corporation waitin' list … but that could take years, so it could! Y'know whit?" she said, her eyes rolling dreamily.

"Whit?" Rasputin asked.

"Ah'd love a hoose in Carntyne," Rita sighed again, "But that's an impossible dream."

"Even a wee tenement somewhere," Rasputin said. "Ah'd live anywhere wi' you ma wee lamb!"

Rita smiled and kissed his cheek.

"Ye need a back-hander or ye've had it," she said sourly. "We canny afford that, Raspy!"

"Ah'll be away maist o' the time, anywey," Rasputin said. "You'll be steyin' wi' yer mammy till ah get hame an' the war's ower," he said.

"Aye, Ah'll stey wi' ma mammy and Uncle Wullie till you get demobbed, Raspy. Aw, it's terrible, int it … this war! Ye WULL come back, Raspy, won't ye?" Rita gripped her husband's hand, almost in panic.

"Don't you worry, hen," Raspy said, showing a stiff upper lip, "There's no' a bullet in this world that'll get me. In fact, when they see me, they'll run for their lives."

"AH nearly did that masel' when Ah first me ye," Rita said.

"But then ye got tae know the inner me, eh?" Raspy smiled.

"Oh aye," Rita sighed and once more softly kissed his cheek.

"We'll manage tae get away for a few days honeymoon next week sometime," Raspy said rubbing their noses together.

"Aye, right enough," Rita said, "It's Hogmanay and everything comes tae a stoap. We might get a few days doon in Saltcoats. Ah think Mrs Cominsky's got a wee single-end there Ah'm sure she'll gie us."

"Aw, that would be great!" Rasputin said, "We could take moonlight strolls intae Ardrossan and back. Just you an' me, haun-in-haun wi' the moonlight strikin' your hair and the lovelight flashin' in yer lovely eyes! It'll be heaven!"

The dreamers sat in their own wonderland corner until Barney stood up and announced:

"Ladies and gentlemen, ra last waltz ..." The Bachles struck up "I'll See You In My Dreams" as the happy couple and their guests took the floor.

Curdy McVey took Annie, Ina and the happy couple back to twenty-seven Well Street. It was still early afternoon and, while Annie put the kettle on, Ina vanished into her own house to prepare her boudoir for the newly weds.

She smoothed out the multi-coloured patchwork quilt her father had loved and Mrs Cominsky had made. Ina McLatchie stepped back and surveyed her work. She had balloons pinned all over the room and notices bawling 'Hard-Up' and 'Good Luck'. She sighed. While she was pleased to hand over her bedroom to Rita and Rasputin, a little pang tweaked her heart and she wished that she was doing it for herself. Still, she thought, she would not give up. Wullie McSorley was just a man ... and all men are vulnerable!

Ina cheered up and humming happily, joined Annie and the lovers for a cup of tea.

Fingers McGeachie had wasted no time in getting about his nefarious work after Wullie had left. His drained bathtub was now slurping with his ten-minute booze.

Fingers began to fill up the 'ginger' bottles he had accumulated, corked them and placed them in a cardboard box. He grimaced as they clinked noisily as he carried them down the stairs and into the back court where he had left his wheelbarrow.

The noise of the 'caurs' trundling along London Road, with their dimmed windows and clanging bells, helped to dampen the sound of the rattling bottles, much to Fingers' relief as he turned down Claythorn Street and on into Stevenston Street. He decided to cut through the pend which connected Stevenston Street and Well Street. The cobbled stones seemed to make the bottles rattle all the more and Fingers' eyes kept sweeping from side-to-side, on the lookout for any foreign bodies...like Erchie McPherson and any others of his ilk.

He had almost reached the the wide exit into Well Street when he heard a slight cough coming from the shadows.

"Ello, 'ello," the familiar voice of Erchie McPherson boomed, "And whit have we here, then, eh?"

Erchie's tin hat glinted in the moonlight as he stepped forward.

"Aw naw, no' again!" Fingers sighed.

"And whit have we here?" Erchie said, peering into the cardboard box.

Fingers pulled a bottle out of the box and handed it to Erchie.

"Have a swig," he said.

"Ah do nut drink on duty," Erchie was adamant. "It is mair than ma life's worth."

"But it's jist lemonade Ah made masel' Ah'm takin' tae the Salvation Army hostel for their Hogmanay," Fingers lied, knowing full well that Erchie would refuse to taste his concoction.

"Oh, we're intae daein' good works noo, are we, Fingers, eh?" Erchie said sarcastically.

"Ye know ma motto, Erchie..."

"Constable McPherson," Erchie said stuffily,

"Aye..er..ye know ma motto, Constable McPherson..."If Ah can help somebody as Ah pass along..."

"Aye, Ah know," Erchie said, "As long as it gies ye a gain," he added. "If you're daein' this for charity, Fingers, pigs might fly."

"Don't mention pigs," Fingers said.

"Right," Erchie said, uncorking the bottle, "let's taste this home-made lemonade." He took a long swig, smacked his lips and drew the back of his hand across his mouth.

"No' bad lemonade that!" he said.

"Nuthin' but the best for the poor and lonely," Fingers said.

"Ye're a' heart, Fingers," Erchie said, taking another swig.

"If Ah can help somebody...." Fingers began.

"As you pass along," Erchie interrupted.

"That's right," Fingers said, "here, have another." Fingers handed Erchie another bottle which the Special Constable took and downed half of it in one single gulp.

"Geez!" Erchie slurred, "that'sh the besht lemonade Ah hiv ever tasted, sho it ish!"

"Good!" Fingers said, "Here, have another." Erchie killed off the other half of the bottle and smacked his lips.

"Ye know Fingersh, Ah am nut completely satisfied that this is merely lemonade. It tastes mair like an alcoholic beverage."

"Would Ah take an alcoholic beverage tae the Salvation Army?" Fingers protested.

"There's word oot that somebody in these parts is tryin' tae dae the Johnny Walker distillery oot o' a joab," Erchie said. "Shomebody has taken it upon themshevels for tae make their ain, special booze....an' Ah think Ah know who that shomebody is!"

"Don't look at me!" Fingers cried.

"Ah am findin' it hard for tae look at ANYBODY!" Erchie said, widening his eyes. "Ah'll have tae arresht ye, Fingersh. Ah'm takin' ye in...'cosh Ah think you're tryin' take take ME in."

Fingers protested but Erchie held up his hand.

"Stoap!" he ordered as though directing traffic, "You, Fingersh, think ye ur somebody just because ye stey up a wally close and have a bath in the hoose.. An' look at me...a special polis attached tae the Eastern Division and makin' sure oor blackoots are in place for when the Jerries come ower. Me, Erchie McPherson who took a German prisoner in the night and who'll nae doot get a commendation frae Mr Sillitoe himsel'. Me, who has tae pull oot an auld zinc bath frae under the bed and place it in front o' the fire and fill kettles o' watter and sit there and waash masel'."

"Well, whit's wrang wi' that? Hunners o' people hiv tae dae that," Fingers said.

"No' wi' their maw sittin three yards away wi' her cronies playin' ponnies at the time," Erchie moaned. "It's no' dignified...especially wi' me wearin' ma official tin hat. It's worse when the wireless strikes up the National Anthem!"

"Well, ye can always go tae the public baths, in Greenheid Street," Fingers offered.

"Ur ye kiddin'?" Erchie cried, "Hiv ye ever tried them, eh? The watter in they places is scaldin'. It could melt iron, Ah'm tellin' ye! Look whit happened tae Big Stumpy McKechnie, six feet two, he was. Ah widnae say that Stumpy suffered wi' verrucas but wan day he went intae the public baths and, bein' a big, careful bloke, he sat at the side o' the bath an' dipped hi feet intae the watter for tae test it."

"Wise man!" Fingers said.

"Aye, ye would think so," Erchie agreed, "But when he walked o they baths he was jist four feet wan."

"His verrucas had vanished?" Fingers asked.

"His feet had vanished," Erchie grimaced.

"Aye, well Ah'm gled Ah don't have tae worry aboot that when Ah want tae clean masel," Fingers said.

"Dae ye use a thermometer?" Erchie asked.

"No jist an ordinary bath," Fingers said. "Here, have another swig."

Erchie took a large gulp and smacked his lips once more in satisfaction.

"Geez, that's powerful stuff, that lemonade!" he said. "It makes me feel at ease wi' the world, know whit Ah mean? Ah'm no' chewin' at the bit any mair."

"It's melted yer heart, Erchie?"

"It's melted ma teeth," Erchie said, taking Fingers by the arm. "Right, c'mon, you're under arrest."

"Aw, hing oan!" Fingers cried and relieved Erchie of his police whistle, which was sticking out of his top pocket. Fingers gave the whistle a few hard blasts and the response was the hurrying feet of Erchie's inspector.

Erchie was now singing loudly 'Mammy' and was down on one knee.

The inspector gave Erchie a clap when he had finished.

"Right, McPherson," the inspector said, putting out his hand and helping him to his feet." "We really don't encourage our men for to serenade the punters while oot on their beat." Turning to Fingers, he said, "Has SPECIAL constable McPherson been annoying you, sir?" he inquired, emphasising the word 'Special'.

"Not at all, sir!" Fingers said, "In fact he was just about for to give me his Harry Lauder impression. But Ah do think that it is ridiculous that oor polismen should be strutting the beat, hauf smugged."

"I agree with you entirely, sir. But Ah do emphasise that he is not wan of us regulars. Right you," he snapped, pulling on Erchie's arm, "Ah'll deal wi' you back at the station. Goodnight sir, and a Happy New Year tae you for when it comes."

"The same tae you, Superintendent," Fingers replied and watched a protesting Erchie being led off towards Tobago Street.

Fingers took a swig from one of the bottles and, whistling merrily, carried on towards Well Street...number twenty-seven.

Ina McLatchie sat alone in her home, her head resting back on the easy chair and her eyes closed. The gentle music of Eric Winstone and his Orchestra wafted across the room.

She rose, walked through to the bedroom and looked down on the large double bed that had been occupied by her father for more than twenty years. Jake McLatchie was gone now. It had been a 'lovely funeral' with messages of condolence from Walt Disney, in Hollywood, and others of that ilk.

"Aw, da'," she found herself saying, "it's always at this time o' the year that memories come flooding back … of those, with us last year, but now gone forever". She dabbed her eyes with her hankie and left the room, closing the door quietly behind her. She poured herself a cup of tea and returned to her chair, closing her eyes once more.

She thought of how Wullie McSorley had collected her dad's ashes from the undertakers and had lost them down the plughole at the Come Inn pub. Of how Wullie had said that Auld Jake was now on his watery way 'Doon the Watter' to Rothesay. Of the mock funeral service as she scattered a pint of soot believing it to be her father, on the window box as was his wish. Of Wullie's rude euolgy when he said; "You loved him when he was a star, though he was rude and curt. We know that you will love him still, though he's just a pile of durt!"

She had wept at the time. But she knew it was Wullie's clumsy way and had long forgiven him. Hadn't he tried to make up for his cack handedness by arranging a little pilgrimage for her. It was just one week ago that he took her down to Central Station where they caught the train for Wemyss Bay, then on to the steamer for Rothesay on the Isle of Bute. Wullie and Ina stood on the deck of the boat, breathing in the cool air and enjoying the sting of the wind against their cheeks. The rolling green hills passed slowly by...another world away from the grime and greyness of Well Street. Wullie took in huge gulps of the clean, fresh air and sniffed the tang of the water...mixed with the oil from the ship's chugging engines. Ina thought back to happier, peaceful times when her mother took her on the boat, all the way from the Broomielaw to Rothesay, where her father was appearing at the Winter Gardens. She recalled the excitement of the journey. Of sailing down the Clyde and of the accordion player on deck encouraging the passengers to sing songs like 'Sailing Doon the Clyde' and 'Goodbye Old Ship of Mine'. Of sweet tea and shortbread 'down below'. Of another life. Wullie had purchased a small wreath from Mary Fox's florist shop, in London Road, before they caught the number twenty-six 'caur' going into the city centre!

Solemnly they walked down to the pebble beach where they stood in silence for a moment, Wullie, had stood, hands crossed and head bowed.

"Would ye say a wee prayer, Wullie?" Ina had asked, dabbing her eyes. Wullie nodded, cleared his throat and said. "We hiv come doon here for tae pray for Jake. It is his daughter's wish. We know that we'll no' see him here, He's been eaten by a fish."

Ina wailed and Wullie put a comforting arm around her shoulder. Ina sniffed, composed herself and stepped slowly forward and threw the wreath into the lapping water.

Seconds later it was back, lying soggy on the beach. Once more Ina threw it into the water and again it was washed up amongst the tangled seaweed. And again Ina threw it in only to see it washed up a dripping mess. By now Ina had thrown all dignity to the wind and her demure stance slipped. Taking a run towards the water, she pitched the messy pulp as hard as she could only to see a swooping, cawing seagull descend and tear what was left of it to pieces.

"Ach," she said, "ma da' wisnae a' that fond o' flooers anywey!"

Wullie and Ina strolled along the prom before crossing the road and on up the small strip of street that was the Gallowgate where Wullie bought two bags of chips, liberally sprinkled with salt and vinegar. They ate the delicacy as they wandered through the popular holiday town...along past the imposing Glenburn Hotel before turning back towards the pier where the steamer awaited them.

The journey back was a replay where they stood on the deck, taking in the fresh, clean air before going below for a cup of hot, sweet tea.

Ina had thanked Wullie for his thoughtfulness and they had arrived home tired but exhilarated.

Ina was brought back from her thoughts by a light tapping on the door. Annie peeked her head round.

"Come on in, Ina," Annie said gently, "ye canny sit in here a' by yersel'...c'mon!"

Ina smiled. Kind Annie! Always there when you needed her! The wireless was on in Annie's house and Chick Henderson was singing 'Begin The Beguine.' Annie had set the table with the currant bun and the ginger wine.

"Sorry, but nae dumplin!" she said.

"Talkin' aboot Rasputin," Wullie said,

"Who's talkin' aboot Rasputin?" Annie snapped, noting Wullie's facetiousness....

"The dumplin'," Wullie said, "Naturally, when ye mentioned dumplin', Ah thought ye was referrin' tae oor genius."

Rasputin, who was sitting at the table reading 'Advanced Geometry" grunted without looking up. He was used to Wullie's snide remarks.

"Ah'm talkin' aboot the dumplin' Ah never got makin' in the wash hoose because o' that German."

"Aye, well don't forget he did oor Rita a favour," Wullie said.

Annie nodded,

"Aye, right enough," she said.

"Ah'll away in and get ready for the bells!" Wullie said, swaggering off.

Rasputin looked up, "Aye ye never know who might walk in on ye?" he said.

"Are ye expectin' anybody special, Raspy?" Annie asked.

Rasputin shrugged.

"Well ye never know," he said, "The king might pop in."

Annie stifled a laugh.

"Ach, don't be daft," she chuckled. "The king probably disnae know where the Calton is....probably disnae even know where Glesca is!"

"Oh aye he definitely does," Rasputin said with conviction.

"How dae you know?" Annie asked, knitting her brows.

"'Cos he showed me his crown and sceptre," Rasputin said.

"How does that tell ye he knows the Calton?"

"'Cos he bought his crown at the Barras," Rasputin said, "He telt me. He said that when he became king, efter his brother chucked it, he found his brother's crown was too big and they didnae have enough money for to buy another wan. So, he made a quick dash up tae Glesca where he heard that you could buy anythin' at the Barras. And that's where he got wan..wi' a sceptre thrown in."

"Ah don't believe it," Annie said.

"It's dead true," Rasputin said, a little hurt "although he wsinae sure o' the genuineness o' the crown until he saw it printed inside it. "The Crown Salerooms, Bath Street," it said. And, oan the sceptre, it said, "as thrown in the air by the leader of the Larkhall Flute Band'."

Annie was quite impressed.

"Did ye hiv an audience?" she asked.

Rasputin shook his head.

"Naw, Ah was jist there masel' although there was some folk hingin' aboot in the palace. Ah was there for tae get ma medal. The king apologised that he had ran oot o' British medals and gied me a German wan that wance belanged tae Santa Claus."

"Ah didnae know Santa Claus was a German!" Annie said, screwing up her nose.

"Oh, aye, " Rasputin said, "Claus is a well known German name."

"He would've got plenty British medals if he'd went roon the Barras," Annie said.

"Can ye get ANYTHIN' roon the Barras?" Rasputin asked.

"Listen son, " Annie said, "Dae ye know wee Aggie McBean?"

Rasputin nodded.

"Well, she went roon the Barras wan Sunday efternoon for a surprise present for her auld faither's birthday. Know whit she came back wi'?"

Rasputin' shook his head once more.

"A wean!" Annie said.

"That would be a surprise for her auld faither!" Rasputin said.

"It was a bigger surprise tae HER," Annie said, "When she left the hoose she wisnae even expectin'."

"That's a load o' rubbish!" Rasputin said.

"It is not!" Annie replied.

"Well," Rasputin said, "it just goes for tae prove that ye can get anythin' at the Barras...and ye meet many famous people there as well!"

Annie threw up her arms.

"Ah've never met any famous people at the Barras...except Irish Paddy who does his Houdini act."

Ina agreed. 'Irish Paddy' could be seen every weekend at the London Road end of the Barras where he would invite his audience to strap him up in a strait jacket and padlock him and he always DID get free with the pennies being tossed into his 'bunnet' and polite applause echoing round the street. Irish Paddy was a 'draw' welcomed by the stall holders.

"Ye'll see mair famous people than Irish Paddy roon the Barras," Rasputin said.

"Who for instance?" Annie demanded to know.

Rasputin thought for a moment, then, snapping his fingers said,

"Well, d'ye know that wee bloke who's got the stall that sells rags? The wan wi' the squashed nose an' nae teeth?"

"He's aboot four feet two?" Annie asked.

Rasputin nodded,

"Aye, that's him?" he said.

"Wee Smelly," Annie said, recognising the description. "He wears the Burma Star oan his greasy lapel?"

"Aye, that's him," Rasputin said. "D'ye know who he REALLY is?"

"Aye, he's Wee Smelly McTavish, frae Montieth Row. His faither used tae have a stall sellin' bric-a-brac."

"Whit was HIS name?" Rasputin asked, narrowing his eyes.

"Big Smelly," Annie said.

"Well you are wrang," Rasputin said. "Wee Smelly is a pseudonym. He is incognito."

"Right, then," Annie said, "Who is he?"

"ERROL FLYNN", Rasputin said with a smug expression.

"Ach, away ye go," Annie retorted, "Errol Flynn..the handsomest man in Hollywood...who's at least six feet tall and has his ain teeth. If Wee Smelly is Errol Flynn, how did he go doon frae six feet tae four feet two?"

"When you THOUGHT Errol was six feet, he was really only four feet two. He wore high platform shoes."

"He must've been wearin' stilts," Annie said.

"They dae things like that in Hollywood," Rasputin said,"They can make ye look like anybody. Did you know that that wisnae a real hump that Charles Laughton had in The Hunchback of Notre Dame?"

"Ah knew it wisnae a wart," Annie said. "Ah suppose it was a cushion?"

"Nope," Rasputin said knowingly, "It was a midget."

"They stuck a midget up his back?" Annie said glancing over at Ina, who giggled.

"Aye, y'see," Rasputin explained, "Charles couldnae remember his lines. So they stuck a midget wi' a script up his back as a prompter. When Charles forgot his lines the wee midget whispered them in his ears."

Annie threw up her arm once more.

"Aw, Raspy, Ah despair o' you. Wee Smelly is really Errol Flynn, Charles Laughton runnin' aroon' wi' a midget up his back. Whit would a big star like Errol Flynn be daein' sellin' rags roon the Barras, eh? Did he go up tae the studio bosses and say, "Unless youse gie me better pictures tae be in Ah am resignin' and settin' up a stall at The Barras. Ah'm handin' in ma platform boots an intend for to go back tae ma original height of four feet two."

"Errol was runnin' away frae an angry faither," Rasputin said.

"That's mair plausable," Annie said, "Some lassie's faither who thought that she had been wranged?"

"Naw, jist an auld bloke that fancied him," Rasputin said.

"Ah've never heard so much rubbish in ma life!" Annie said, "Ah always looked on you as a genius, Raspy. Then ye come oot wi' a' that crap."

"You'd be surprised whit's goin' on roon aboot ye," Raspy said, "And Ah AM a genius. Who dae ye think invented the telephone, eh?"

"Alexander Graham Bell," Annie answered.

"Ah know," Rasputin said.

"Let's talk aboot somethin' sensible," Annie sighed, "Ye'll be happy noo that ye're married eh?"

"Aw, aye!" Rasputin' said, "Ma maw said it's a fine institution. She said she would've married ma faither only she couldnae bear tae look at him every day in that stinkin', drunken stupor."

Rasputin wearily shook his head.

"Yer da' was always in a drunken stupor?" Annie asked sympathetically.

"Naw, she was," Rasputin replied.

Rita, who had been silent during the discourse between her mother and fiancé, piped up.

"Ah didnae like the idea o' you walkin' doon the aisle wearin' a parachute," Rasputin said. "Wan gust o' wind an' ye could've ended up zoomin' back doon the aisle and oot the door."

Wullie stepped back and looked at himself in the mirror. His chest puffed out with pride. His Highland Light Infantry uniform still fitted him after all these years. He still looked resplendent in his McKenzie tartan kilt Aye, he was a fine figure of a man, he decided!

He remembered his first leave from the regiment 'way back in 1915. Soon he would be leaving for France and the front line. But, before embarkation, they were given leave. Before going off to war, Wullie had eyes for Sadie McGinty, the beauty of Claythorn Street. He was a 'midgie man' then and, despite his nightly encounter with the zinc bath, from under the bed, he reeked of carbolic. Scented soap was a luxury for others. The odour did not mix well with Sadie's cheap scent, purchased in the local chemist shop when she could afford it.

Wullie never noticed the mixing of the smells as Sadie always, despite her scent, smelled of cough sweeties she purchased regularly at Glickman's shop, in London Road. Not that Sadie had a chronic cough. She just liked the taste of the Glickman's popular sweeties where a queue of children, from St Alphonsus' Primary School, just across the road could always be seen at 'dinner time'. Wullie's heart fluttered everytime he met Sadie.

But Sadie McGinty had other ideas. She had an eye for Wee Hughie Broon, a tram driver on the Yellow 'caur' Bellahouston run. It was Hughie's smart, green uniform that attracted her, Wullie was sure of that.

But he had to admit that the wee man was always well turned out, spotless with his white, stiff collar and the dark green tie of the Glasgow Corporation Transport Department.

The fact that he was toothless didn't seem to bother Sadie. For it WAS the uniform that caught her lovely eye. Wullie had even seen her turn round when a postman passed by. Yes, it was the uniform. He could only smile. Which, he reckoned, was more than Hughie Broon could do.

Wullie had arrived home on the Saturday morning and was on a week's leave. That night he had stepped out and marched smartly down London Road, towards Claythorn Street, his kilt swaying from side -to- side in the soft breeze, his brass buttons gleaming like twenty-two carat gold.

It was 'by chance' that he bumped into Sadie McGinty, who was coming out of Craig's fish and chip shop where she had been purchasing a tuppenny bag of chips for her mother and a pudding supper for her father.

"Ooh!" Sadie had exclaimed when she saw Wullie dressed like the professional warrior that he now was.

Hughie Broon was quickly forgotten and Wullie and Sadie had danced the night away at the Calton Social Club hall. They had spent the entire week together enjoying themselves. The Queens Theatre, in Watson Street, at Glasgow Cross, was always packed for their vaudeville programmes. And The Geggie cinema, in Kirkpatrick Street, had all the latest silents from Hollywood.

The week's furlough passed quickly and, on the last night, Wullie had taken Sadie to the Glasgow Pavilion Theatre, in Renfield Street, to see Ella Shields, knocking them in the aisle with her famous rendition of 'Burlington Bertie'. And there was 'Little Tich' clowning around in his four-feet long shoes.

Afterwards, they had gone for a fish tea, in Sauchiehall Street and the day was rounded off by adjourning to the back of Sadie's close, in Claythorn Street, for a last 'winchin' session.

They stood, gazing lovingly into each other's eyes for hours, only to be interrupted by some brat hurrying up the close after seeing a Lon Chaney film that had frightened the life out of him. "Oh-PEN, PEE-EN" was the terrified cry as the scared 'wean' dashed up the stairs, not wanting to linger at the door in case the 'Claw' caught up with him.

Sadie swore undying love for Wullie, who suddenly felt like William the Conqueror. Between passionate kisses, Sadie would pop a cough sweetie into her mouth and Wullie wondered how their romance would go when, after the war, he reverted to his 'midgie man's' dungarees and, instead of the sharp clean smell of brassoed buttons, he would, once more stink of back court middens.

He quickly shoved such thoughts to one side. Sadie loved him and promised to wait for him when HE promised HER that he would come marching home with at least one Victoria Cross...received for valour on the battlefield.

Sadie had cooed with delight and pressed her kiss hard against Wullie's eager lips for a good five minutes and twenty-four seconds.

"Ah'll be waitin' for you, Wullie, no matter how long it takes," Sadie purred just as her mother's rasping voice echoed down the stair- well ordering, "Get up these stairs this minute!".

When the Great War was over Wullie had come home with a chipped thigh bone where a German sniper had grazed him. Sadie, he learned, was now married...to Wee Hughie Broon.

Hughie had acquired a new set of gleaming teeth and had won her over with his smile. Also, he was now an inspector on the 'caurs' with a fancier uniform. Wullie had gone off women forever.

With one last, pleased, look in the mirror, he turned and entered the room .

"Ooh!" Ina said, "ye look wonderful, Wullie. Ye should wear yer uniform a' the time."

"Ah wish Ah could and get ower there an' gie them a bloody nose like Ah did the last time." he snarled.

"Well," Rasputin said, "if ye know how tae go an elephant, Ah could put a good word in for ye wi' Monty."

Wullie threw him a look of contempt. He was secretly pleased that Ina had noticed his smart appearance but was careful not to sit too near.

Annie poured out tea and they sat in silence. Wullie wondered if Fingers had managed to get his pipes working and Annie wondered how Big Sammy was getting on in the jungle.

Curdy McVey said nothing. He thought about the old woman he had sat up with all night. The noble profession of undertaking was not one of his own choosing. His mother feared his father was dying of alcohol poisoning, after one night finding her tin of Brasso empty and her man lying on the linoleum frothing at the mouth and smiling with newly acquired twenty-carat gold teeth.

She had spotted an advertisment in the Evening Citizen for an apprentice undertaker and immediately packed Curdy, newly left school, down to Hector McSween's ('It disnae matter where they've been, they'll be planted well by Auld McSween') funeral parlour.

She saw the opportunity for a cut-price funeral and sent Curdy packing along for the interview. He got the job but wished he had gone for a more established firm like Frank Crum or Mathew Bones, both in Bridgeton looking after both catholics and protestants. Anyway, he got the job with Hector McSween and his first assignment was to collect old Jake McLatchie. This was the call that would acquaint him with Wullie McSorley, who he mistook for the corpse that day.

He felt that he could better himself and that Hector McSween was a cheap-skate. He first suspected his employer of skulduggery, which he thought was an apt word, when putting a corpse in an expensive forty-two pounds coffin and saw, stamped inside "Californian Oranges". McSween explained this away by saying the dead man was the American president of the Orange Order in Calton. Curdy believed him because he wanted to. But when he saw another dead man being laid into a coffin with the word "PINEAPPLE" stencilled on it with McSween saying the man was the president of the Calton Branch of the Knights of Saint Columba and the coffin was destined for 'St Alphonsus' Pineapple, in London Road, he began to suspect even more.

As fate would have it, Curdy's father did not succumb to his Brasso swallowing. He died later under the hooves of a coal horse.

But Curdy had found a friend in Wullie and Annie. He had offered Rita half-a-dozen second-hand shrouds to make her wedding dress but she declined, facetiously saying she wouldn't be found dead in them.

He was alone in the world now. After his father died, his mother ran away with a Russian sardine fisherman and had taken to heavy drinking. He was told on good authority the pair were canned every other night...well oiled! He was glad his father was not around to see this as he would certainly have turned in his grave...a grave he would have got cut price by his adoring son.

His thoughts were interrupted by the noise of Wullie's medals clinking. He looked up and saw Wullie posing at the doorway.

"Geez!" he exclaimed, "Ye look like General Gordon, Wullie!" he said with admiration.

Wullie smiled broadly. Ina McLatchie, too, was taken by Wullie's appearance.

"Ye look just like Errol Flynn," she said.

"The six feet tall wan or the four feet two wan?" Wullie grunted.

"Just like in "They Died Wi' Their Boots On," she added.

Yes, he's a fine looking man, Ina thought! She wondered if she would ever get married? It had been all part of her plans when she left Charlotte Street School all those years ago. To find a good job and, after a while find a good husband. Wullie McSorley had always appealed to her despite his grumpiness. But things never work out to plan.

She got a job in Templeton's carpet factory, in Bridgeton, and stayed there for most of her working life....until old Jake fell ill and had to be cared for. Then she had to give up work and devote her life to him. But it had been a good life...better than most, and she was thankful for that.

The girls at the factory were a cheery crowd and there was always plenty going on. While most of them favoured the swinging Barrowland Ballroom, she prefered the more sedate Dennistoun Palais where she waltzed and quick-stepped to the sound of Laurie Blandford and His Broadcasting Band.

There were holidays in Rothesay when old Jake was booked in at The Winter Gardens where he did his monologues. And then came the big one. Jake was offered a film role, in Hollywood, to appear with the great dog actor, Rin-Tin-Tin. She was just a wee girl then but she remembered the excitement as they caught the train for Southampton and boarded the huge liner which would take them to New York. Then on to an aeroplane and across the three-thousand miles of America.

This would be something to tell the kids back home. To fly in an aeroplane was an experience for someone in another world. Back home the only aeroplane anyone saw was droning and flying over Well Street where excited children looked up, pointed to the sky and echoed.. "Look! An airy!" Now she had actually been up in one. She would tell them all about it when she got home and watch their faces turn green.

The excitement never left her as she was pitched into the great celluloid world of faces she had only seen in the Arcadia Cinema, in London Road. Jackie Coogan and Jackie Cooper, Gloria Swanson and Tom Mix, her favourite cowboy. Lon Chaney, who sent shivers up spines all over the world and who sat her on his knee and whom she could never be afraid of again. And, of course, Rin-Tin-Tin himself ....a canine her father couldn't stand because of its toilet manners and its attraction to his left leg.

The whole adventure was a trip to heaven and, when she arrived home, she spent every minute of her free time telling her story over and over again to her pals, who sat mouths open, on the stairs of her tenement home. Old Jake was treated as a celebrity when he arrived back in Glasgow. He made all of page five in The Sunday Post and had barely got in the door when he was offered a week at the Glasgow Metropole, in Stockwell Street. It was a famous theatre he knew well and, while in Hollywood, he had spent many a night chatting to another big star who also knew and loved 'The Met'. Stan Laurel talked and talked of his Metropole memories.

It all seemed another lifetime ago. She DID have opportunities to marry but the idea was out of the question while her ailing father depended on her. But she DID have an eye for Wullie McSorley, next door, although her attentions were not reciprocated. And, when Old Jake died and Wullie had taken care of the funeral arrangements, she thought there might be a chance for some happiness. And there did seem to be when, on the night of Wullie's niece, Rita's, engagement to Rasputin Plunkett, Wullie had actually squeezed her hand while they were in the air-raid shelter during a raid. But Wullie had gone back to his old ways. The war, of course, had knocked everybody off track. She cursed it and hoped only that one day Wullie McSorley would squeeze her hand once again. Now here he was looking every inch the hero and a new year about to begin. She wondered if this would be the year when peace would come to them?

Annie noticed Ina deep in thought and broke in.

"Ah jist hope we get through the night withoot an air-raid!" she said.

"Aye, well Fat Goering'll dae anythin' tae spoil oor enjoyment," Wullie answered.

"Ah wonder if they celebrate it up there," Ina said, nodding towards the ceiling.

"Up where?" Wullie asked.

"Up there," Ina repeated. "Where ma faither is."

"It could be doon there," Wullie said, pointing to the floor. "Ah would definitely think they would be gettin' stuck intae it doon there. Auld Nick will have mair bevvy than he knows whit tae dae wi'."

"He should," Annie said, "efter a' that's where it originated."

"Are you suggestin' that booze was created in Hell?" Wullie gasped.

"Where else?" Annie said, "it's a curse...an' ye don't get curses in Heaven."

"Aye, well, thanks tae Jimmy Smith, Ah'll no' be daein' much cursin' the night!" Wullie moaned. "Hauf a boattle!" he added, shaking his head sadly.

"Aye, Ah dae think they'll be celebratin' up there, Ina," Annie said, "but probably wi' ambrosia."

"Wullie's brows shot up.

"Ye mean they're a' gonny bring in the new year wi' a plate o' RICE?" he cried.

"Ambrosia is the drink of the gods," Annie said smugly.

"Ambrosia is tinned rice," Wullie snapped, "And there's only WAN God and it's NECTAR he'll be drinkin'...if anybody wull be bringin' in the new year wi' rice, it'll be your Sammy."

"Yer auld man'll no' get stoned on nectar, that's for sure," Wullie said, turning to Ina, "An' Ah don't suppose he'll be too happy at hivin' tae bring in hogmanay wi' an insipid beverage an' a plate o' tinned rice."...

"AMBROSIA!" Wullie frowned. "It's jist as well that your idea disnae catch on," he said to Annie, "Imagine First Fittin' anybody, gettin' greeted at the door and ushered in and, there ye are wishin' everybody a happy new year. Ye stick yer airm intae yer cairry-oot bag and pull oot a tin o' rice... 'Voila', ye say!

"an' here's a tin o' creamola for chasers...ye'd be chased oot the hoose."

"And that's maybe no' a bad thing!" Annie said.

Wullie shrugged.

"If yer da' IS up there," he said to Ina, " and he starts tae sing, hauf the angels in Heaven'll ask for a transfer."

"Ma faither was a good singer," Ina said huffily, "He couldnae sing in the bath 'cos we didnae hiv wan. But he used tae sing in the toilet."

"Oh, ye don't need tae tell me that!" Wullie exclaimed, "Ye could never get intae that stairheid lavvy for him singin'. When he went in there ye couldnae get him oot. Ah don't mind a wee, quick song. But wi' him it was a whole opera. Ah wance went doon an' had tae staun on the landin for nearly three 'oors till he finished.. Il Travatore, it was. It should've been Il Lavatory..no' only that he sang the soprano's part."

"Ah've never heard such rubbish in ma life!" Annie snapped,

"Oh, you heard him an' a'?" Wullie cried.

"Ah'm gonny sing a song," Curdy interrupted.

"On ye go, son," Annie said.

"Right, Ah'm away oot on the prowl," Wullie said. "Ah've had enough sufferin' the night."

Wullie straightened his hat and swaggered out with a cheery wave. "Ah might just be yer First Foot," he called.

Curdy cleared his throat and, standing up with his arms outstretched, began. "I aint got nobody, and nobody got me..." he chorused.

"Aw, that's enough o' that!" Annie said, "ye don't have tae bring yer work intae the hoose."

Curdy shut his mouth and, huffily, crossed his arms.

Wullie stepped out of the close and took in a deep breath of the cool night air. He could hear singing coming from some of the houses where early revellers had begun.

The sound swelled his heart. He wished only that Adolph Hitler could stroll through Calton with him. The cheery sound of singing coming from behind blacked-out windows would have scotched his belief that the Glasweigans, like the Londoners, or the folk from Coventry, were being 'cowed'. That morale was rock bottom and the fight in them gone. It was Hogmanay, a very special day in the Glasgow calendar and a day that was not going to be snatched from them. The Luftwaffe's bombs were forgotten and it made Wullie proud to be a native of this no mean city..and to be a Scottish soldier.

He strolled down the length of the street and, hearing the sound of raucous singing coming from the Come Inn Pub, he crossed the street and walked into the smokey din of the revelling crowd. Jimmy Smith spotted him and, pushing his way through the crowd, grabbed him by the arm and steered him towards the bar.

"First time Ah've seen ye wi' the gear oan, Wullie," he said with admiration.

"Don't you talk tae me!" Wullie snapped.

"Och c'mon, Wullie. There's a war on. But seein' ye there, that proud in yer uniform, Ah don't think it matters whit war ye fought in. Ye're a true Scottish Soldier and, in ma book, that entitles ye tae a wee bit o' favouritism....here, stick that in yer sporran."

Jimmy Smith shoved a half bottle of Bells whisky down a surprised Wullie's sporran.

"And ye can have that on the house," Jimmy said.

"Aw, ye're no' a bad sowel efter a', Jimmy!" Wullie said, pumping Jimmy's hand. "Ah'll drink yer health the night..efter the bells."

Jimmy slapped Wullie on the shoulder and set up a pint which he slid over the counter.

"On the house," he said.

Sanity had returned to the world, Wullie thought. He now had two half bottles. That would allow one visitor an eye-dropper ful. Still, there was always Fingers McGeachie...he hoped!

Wullie stayed in the pub for a while, joining in the singing of 'Bless 'em All' and 'Roll Out The Barrel' and all the oldies. He left the chorus behind him and walked along Stevenston Street towards Kent Street.

The 'Barras' had gone for the night. The large, empty expanse of where they had been lay before him. He stood, silent for a moment, under the bright moonlight and listened. There was no drone of the German air-force's Heinkels...yet. All he heard was the ghostly echo of the traders' voices..'Curtains, Missus....five bob a pair'..'Get yer linoleum here...just imported frae Germany. This linoleum wance graced Hitler's single-end...c'mon, noo, just hauf-a-croon a yerd'.

He turned and walked down to the Gallowgate and up towards Bain Square. The 'Mussel Shoap' was shut at this time of the night but he could still smell the pungent odour of dulse. And memories came too, of Sunday afternoons sitting in the tiled shop eating a plateful of steaming hot mussels, still in their shells and sprinkled with salt and vinegar. "A treat fit for a king," Wullie always thought. And, before leaving the shop, purchasing a bag of 'wulks' supplied with the very necessary pin attached to the brown poke.

These were in better days and Wullie thanked God that HE had placed him in such a wonderful spot to live out his life.

He walked on past the Rapid cycle shop which he remembered had all the latest gleaming bikes in its windows.

He crossed the Square, going through the children's swings where the police box was and where the bomb had dropped leaving a huge, gaping crater a double -decker bus could have fitted into...right outside the small Church of Scotland.

He remembered the night that bomb had dropped. With Annie and Ina and the other neighbours in the street, including the ubiquitous mouth organ player, they were in the air-raid shelter up the pend when the blast shook the dust from the roof. Wullie was sure that their two-storey tenement had been flattened but, after the all clear, they were relieved to see that not even a window had been shattered. The folk in Gallowgate had not been so lucky. The blast of the bomb was directed away from Well Street and had gone towards Gallowgate...shattering scores of windows in its path.

Wullie remembered that, at daylight, with half the children in the street, he went up to inspect 'the Hole'. Some of the children were foraging for shrapnel and now and then a cry of triumph would echo up from the deep aperture and a grimy-faced 'wean' would appear, clutching a lump of silver metal in his mitts.

The hole had been quickly filled in by the authorities and Wullie was now walking across where it had been.

The singing got louder as he approached Well Street. Arriving at number twenty-seven, he looked up. The moon was full. It was a bomber's moon and Wullie wondered if they would have visitors that night? And he didn't mean first footers. He climbed the stairs and was glad to note that Curdy McVey was not singing.

Erchie McPherson left Tobago Street police office after getting a dressing down by his inspector... He was quite sober and the officer-in-charge had accepted Erchie's word that what he had consumed WAS what he thought was home made lemonade. His 'arrest' of the German pilot earlier on in the evening had gone down well with the Eastern Division Chief.

And, not only did Erchie's chest puff out three inches at his superior's applause, it went out even further when he was commanded to appear before Percy Sillitoe, the Chief Constable of Glasgow, to receive an award for his bravery in capturing the German bomber pilot. Erchie would be hard to live with from this moment on!

He walked along towards Well Street. The Calton Social Club was closed although some of the 'coarner boys' still hung around outside. Erchie moved them on. Mary Welsh's shop, next door, was still open and a few customers were inside. Erchie walked on, his eyes sweeping the street for the slightest chink of light coming from a careless window. There was none...only happy singing coming from the houses. He listened carefully for the trundling sound of a wheelbarrow but there was none. Fingers McGeachie must be doing a detour, he reckoned. But he would catch him, he had no doubts about that. He would visit Annie's later on.

Peter Rossi's ice cream cafe, in London Road, was still open and the clear tenor voice of Beniamino Gigli came out in spurts and in between passing, clangin 'caurs'. Erchie continued with his patrol, moving on a drunk man lying across Galbraith's doorway and another outside Latimer's shop, where folk went to get their accumulators charged up for their wire-less sets. Many an accident had happened from splashing acid by hurry-ing 'weans'carrying the accumulators for recharging at sixpence a time.

There was no sign of Fingers and Erchie made his way to number twen-ty-seven.

Nearing the top of the stairs, he could hear Curdy McVey's voice boom-ing out with 'Tip Toe through the Graveyard with Me.' He smiled.

"It's yersel', Erchie!" Annie said, opening the door widely.

Erchie removed his tin hat and entered.

"Quiet night!" he said. "Ah think Jerry must be hivin' the night off!" he added.

"Well Ah hope so!" Annie said.

Wullie came in from the room and Erchie stood up and gaped.

"My, MY!" he said, "Would ye look at that. Ye're a sight for sore eyes, Wullie...Magnificent!"

"Aye, we were a' proud o' oor uniforms then," Wullie said.

"Aye, Ah must admit," Erchie said, "Ye must've been a fine bunch o' men."

"Ye should see his underwear!" Annie said.

"Ah do nut wear underwear with this uniform," Wullie snapped.

"Ooh!" Ina cooed.

"We were the terror o' the Germans," Wullie said, "Ah picked up a Military Medal at the Somme, so Ah did."

"Ah didnae know that!" Annie said in admiration.

"Aye", Wullie went on, "Ah was in this wee cafe and jist looked doon and there it was..lyin' under a table."

"Ah thought ye meant that ye earned it", Annie said in disappointment.

"Ah they didnae want tae gie me too many medals," Wullie said, "it was bad for morale. The Military Medal right efter ma Victoria Cross would've been jist too much."

"Ye never got the Victoria Cross," Annie snapped.

"Aye, that's another medal they didnae dare gie me...although Ah DID destroy a tank. Ah saw this tank goin' across No-Man's land and Ah dashed oot right in front o' it and Blew the tracks right aff, so it did. That was it oot o' action and just staunin' there vulnerable."

"Ye should've definitely got the Victoria Cross for that action, Wullie," Erchie said. "Whit DID ye get?"

"Six months detention," Wullie said, "It was wan o' oors."

"Ach, we a' make mistakes, Wullie," Erchie commiserated.

"It was a different kind o' war then, "Wullie went on, "We used tae staun' there in the trench and have tae black oor face up. Although some o' the mair clatty wans didnae have tae dae that. That trench had mair Jolson impersonators than Elsie Kelly had in her discoveries, Ah'm tellin' ye. When the whistle blew for tae go ower the top, we a' dashed ower tae a quick chorus o' California Here I Come. The Jerries didnae know whether tae shoot or applaud."

Annie poured out more tea.

"We'll get somethin' stronger efter the bells," she said by way of mitigation.

Wullie frowned. He wondered what was keeping Fingers?

Everybody looked up as an authoritative rap at the door broke the silence.

"Ah'll get it," Annie said vanishing into the lobby.

They heard a muffled conversation and the clinking of bottles as Fingers McGeachie entered carrying a large cardboard box which he placed on top of the table.

"Happy New Year everybody," he cried.

Erchie jumped to his feet but Wullie moved quickly and pushed him down on to the chair.

"Just relax, Erchie," Wullie said, "Ye're a guest in this hoose."

"Ye're a bit early wi' yer greetings, Fingers," Annie said, "but ye know ye're always welcome."

Wullie dug into the box and pulled out an Iron Brew bottle which he immediately uncorked.

"Ah, Ah see ye got the iron brew, Fingers!" he said.

Fingers nodded.

"Aye," he said, "it arrived by tube." They laughed.

"Let's taste that," Erchie said grabbing the bottle from Wullie. He took a long swig and smacked his lips.

"It's the best Iron Brew Ah've ever tasted," Erchie said, wiping his lips with the back of his palm. Wullie and Fingers laughed and handed Erchie a bottle which he began to demolish.

"Youse a' know ma motto," Fingers said, "Whitever ye need, ye jist hiv tae cry it, and know, ma freens, that Ah'll supply it."

Rita kissed Fingers lightly on the cheek.

"Aw Fingers," she said, "ye're always there when we need ye. Ma engagement ring an' everything. If Rasputin hadnae asked me first...?

Fingers shook his head.

"Naw, ye're daein' the right thing, hen!" he said. "Ah'm just an ordinary idiot. Rasputin's a professor."

"The King an' Queen like me," Rasputin offered. Erchie was now on to his second bottle.

"Wull Ah gie youse a song?" he asked.

"If ye must," Wullie said.

"Ah wull sing the polis song frae Silbert and Gullivan," he said, bending his knees and going into the song. Erchie finished on a flat note and took another swig at his bottle. Then, remembering his duty, he staggered over to the window.

"Ah'd better check yer blind," he said, pulling in his chest and drawing himself up to his full height.

"Jerry can see a light at ten thousand feet, y'know," he added, turning at the window.

"Well, ye'd better cover yer nose," Annie said.

"Ah'm surprised they let ye oot, Erchie," Fingers said, "the last time Ah saw ye, ye were bein' marched aff tae Tobago Street."

Erchie tapped the side of his nose.

"Ah hiv been commanded for to appear before Mr Sillitoe next week for to receive an award for capturing that German pilot," he said pompously.

"Is it no' the other wey aroon'?" Fingers said.

"It was ME that took him in and that's a' that matters," Erchie said proudly, adding, "Ah would not be surprised if they make me a peer!"

"Ah wish they'd make ye bloody Disappear," Fingers sniped.

Erchie ignored the remark; NOTHING would tarnish his glory this night.

Fingers turned to Rita

"Where ye gonny live noo that ye're married, Rita?" he asked.

"Ah canny afford key money for a factor," Rita sighed.

"We were gonny live wi' ma maw," Rasputin volunteered, "but we chinged oor minds."

"How was that?" Fingers asked.

"She got evicted last week," Rasputin said.

The wailing sound of an air-raid siren screamed over the street.

"Aw, naw!" Annie said, "no' the night, surely? Gie's a break!"

Erchie pulled back the blind and threw the window up. He leaned out and shook his fist at the sky.

"Come doon and fight us face tae face, ya bampots," Erchie bawled.

"Erchie..THE BLINDS...THE BLINDS..!" Annie screamed.

"Ach tae hell wi' the blinds!" Erchie snapped.

Wullie dragged the protesting Erchie in from the window and closed the blinds.

"Come on in, they might hear ye," he said.

Annie sat down and defiantly folded her arms.

"Ah am not goin' doon tae that air-raid shelter," she said, "no' on Hogmanay."

"That goes for me, tae!" Rasputin said.

"If you went doon in that gear ye'd get lynched," Wullie snapped.

"You ur talkin' aboot ma man's weddin' uniform," Rita snapped.

"His weddin' uniform could end up bein' his funeral uniform," Wullie retorted.

Fingers handed Erchie another bottle.

"C'mon, drink up, Erchie," he said.

"Constable McPhershon, if you please," Erchie corrected.

"Aye, Constable McPherson, drink up, ye're in yer aunty's."

Erchie hiccuped twice.

"Ah do not indulge while Ah'm on duty," he said, "But seein' this is jist iron brew...ta!"

He guzzled the lot.

Fingers poured out drinks for everybody.

"Noo, haud on tae yer drinks," he said, "it'll soon be the bells."

Annie brought the corner of her 'peeny' up to her face and dabbed the corner of her eye. She sat staring straight ahead. Rita immediately came over to her side and knelt down. She put a comforting arm around her mother's shoulder.

"Whit is it, mammy?" she said softly.

Annie sniffed, and said, "Och, Ah'm jist thinkin' o' yer faither away in the other side o' the world...a prisoner in this damned war.

"Ah miss him awfu', Rita. Ah can only hope and pray that he's copin' an' that we'll be together soon again...as a family."

"Ah'm sure we will, Mammy!" Rita said. "Try no' tae fret! There's a lot o' wimmen in the same position."

"Ah know, hen, Ah know," Annie sniffed, "but Ah canny help it."

Fingers switched on the wireless in time to hear the last chords of music being played.

In best BBC English the announcer said: "...And that was Jack Hylton and his Orchestra. And now...standby ..."

A hush fell over the house until shattered by the striking of Big Ben...The bell echoed around the house and Fingers was the first to cry out... "A Happy New Year tae Everybody..." He kissed Annie first and then Ina and Rita. Everybody kissed everybody and then clinked glasses. The Pipes and Drums of the Glasgow Police Band set the mood going and all sang, with gusto, 'A Guid New Year..ta ane an' a'...'

Fingers went round filling and spilling the glasses.

Wullie grabbed Ina and swung her on to the middle of the floor. Putting his hand into his sporran he pulled out a rubber fish and handed it to her.

"Here," he laughed, "Nae need for you tae go fishin', Ina...nae need at a'!"

Ina laughed heartily.

"That's whit Ah've been ANGLIN' for , Wullie!" she giggled.

Annie held up her glass..."PEACE THIS YEAR!" she called. Everybody repeated it.."PEACE!...PEACE!....PEACE!"

The merriment was halted by a sharp, loud rap on the door.

"Oh, oor First Fit!" Annie exclaimed. "Ah hope it's somebody tall an' Dark!"

"Ah'll get it!" Rasputin said, going into the lobby.

Muffled voices could be heard coming from the lobby. Everyone looked expectantly at the door. Rasputin entered.

"It's a big monkey," he said.

"Thank God it's no' an elephant!" Wullie said.

Rasputin held the door open wide. A large 'gorilla' strode in. Everybody's mouth fell open.

"A happy new year everybody," the 'gorilla' said, sweeping Annie up into his arms and planting a kiss on her lips. The 'gorilla' stood back and pulled the mask from his head. There was a stunned silence and then happy recognition lit up Annie's face.

"SAMMY!" she cried.."Oh, Sammy...Ma Sammy!" she cried, throwing her arms around his neck and bursting into delirious tears.

"Ah took the right turnin' this time, Annie," Sammy laughed. "Ah was King Kong in the camp's pantomime and escaped intae the jungle."

"Oh Sammy, it must've been a horrendous ordeal for ye, goin' through the jungle!" Annie said.

"Aye, well, Ah nearly got engaged twice tae two amorous gorillas that fancied me," Sammy laughed.

"How did ye get oot o' that situation?" Annie asked worriedly.

"Ah jist telt them Ah was already merried," Sammy chuckled, kissing her once more.

"Oh, ya cheeky monkey!" Annie laughed, hugging him tightly.

"Oh, Annie," Sammy said softly,"Ah'd forgotten how lovely ye are!"

Annie wiped the tear from her eye. "Oh Sammy!" she sighed. Rita threw her arms round her father's neck and hugged him tightly. Annie raised her glass. "Peace this year," she said, "May a' the boys come hame soon and here's a cup tae a' the boys who'll no' come hame. Ah've been blessed this night. Ma man's hame, safe an' sound. We're a faimily again!"

The drone of the Heinkel bombers, on the their way home was drowned out by the singing and jollity coming from the house at 27 Well Street, Calton, near the Barras and from behind every other blacked-out window in the Calton including the packed air-raid shelter 'up the pen'...and every other street in Glasgow, too.

'We'll tak a cup o' kindness yet...For Auld Lang Syne...'

ENDS

Also by James Barclay

PARAS OVER THE BARRAS

There's a war on and for Glasgow, like the rest of Britain, that means air raids, black-outs, food rationing, barrage balloons and the pain of parting as husbands and fathers go off to fight.

For the McSorleys and their neighbours in the East End tenements it is a case of making the best of what life has to offer. This is their laugh-a-line story capturing all the wit and spirit of city life during the dark days of the forties when the grit and humour of Glaswegians overcame all adversities.

James Barclay has created a marvellous range of characters-

Wullie McSorley, a waspish whinger full of biting wit;

His long suffering sister Annie whose man 'Big Sammy' is away fighting;

Her daughter Rita a no-nonsense clippie on the tram caurs;

Her fiance, Rasputin Plunkett, a genius-cum-idiot;

Ina McLatchie, East End Spinster, whose advances on Wullie are continually spurned;

Auld McPhee the grocer who becomes a groper when food coupons are in short supply;

Fingers McGeaghie, the local wide boy who does a nice line in rings – engagement rings, masonic rings, even gas rings.

His arch enemy Erchie McPherson. Erchie is a plumber by day but dictator by night when he puts on his tin hat and becomes a special constable patrolling the beat without fear or favour.

Curdy McVey, the apprentice undertaker, who has a lot to learn about life...

Madame Wee Nellie, coiffeuse el brilliant, who is not all that she seems...

And a motley crew of others including of course the ubiquitous drunk.

The characters are fictitious but the names of shops, streets, tram routes and other locations are just as they were in the forties, evoking a wonderful nostalgic picture of the Glasgow we used to know.

ISBN 1-85217-013-1

9 781852 170134

Also by James Barclay

Andra Thomson is back! The hilarious bigot whose greatest wish to be buried in the hallowed turf of Ibrox Park is rebuffed by the Rangers board...as are his efforts to join the Orange "Ludge" and the Freemasons.

His long-suffering wife, Annie, a devout Catholic, tolerates him...and struggles to keep him in his place.

And his wee pal, Hughie Broon, can see no wrong in those blue ..true blue.. eyes... sometimes bleary from extended visits to McDougal's hostelry.

And who, Andra wonders, is this stranger his lovely daughter, Jean, is going out with. Does he kick with the proper foot?

And Peter, his son, is that the 'Hoarses' he's studying. . . . or what?

This is Glasgow humour at its best and James Barclay has novelised his award-winning play, The Bigot, originally produced and starring Scots actor, Andrew Keir, at Glasgow's Pavilion Theatre.

The one-liners come fast and furious and it all sets out to prove that we are all 'Jock Thamson's Bairns'.

It's another triumph for Glasgow journalist and writer James Barclay, author of the Best Seller 'Paras Over The Barras'...

You'll laugh . . . . and laugh . . . . and laugh again!

"One of the funniest to come our way in a very long time" . . . . The Evening Times.

"It's a long time since I heard an audience laugh so much" . . . . The Sunday Mail.

"Thousands went home to soothe their aching ribs and tell their friends that they haven't laughed so much in years." . . . . Scottish Daily Express.

"Keir finds a winner" . . . . The Glasgow Herald.

ISBN 1-85217-016-6

9 781852 170165